FROM THIN AIR

This Large Print Book carries the
Seal of Approval of N.A.V.H.

FROM THIN AIR

A BLACK SWAN HISTORICAL ROMANCE

CAROLYN BROWN

THORNDIKE PRESS
A part of Gale, Cengage Learning

GALE
CENGAGE Learning

Detroit • New York • San Francisco • New Haven, Conn • Waterville, Maine • London

GALE
CENGAGE Learning™

LIBRARY OF CONGRESS CATALOGING-IN-PUBLICATION DATA

Brown, Carolyn, 1948–
   From thin air / by Carolyn Brown.
      p. cm. — (Thorndike Press large print gentle romance) (A black swan historical romance series ; no. 2)
   ISBN-13: 978-1-4104-2375-7 (alk. paper)
   ISBN-10: 1-4104-2375-1 (alk. paper)
    1. Veterans—Fiction. 2. Arkansas—Fiction. 3. Large type books. I. Title.
PS3552.R685275F76 2010
813'.54—dc22
                                      2009044925

Published in 2010 by arrangement with Thomas Bouregy & Co., Inc.

To my editor, Faith Black.
Thanks for all you do!

CHAPTER ONE

Ira was dead.

The government said so and they didn't lie. So how in the world did he appear from thin air in the Black Swan Hotel and break Alice's fall from the ladder? She blinked several times and stared at him with big green eyes. Maybe she'd died in the fall and he was merely there to escort her into the next life, but surely God wouldn't make a mistake that huge. Ira'd been engaged to her older sister, Catherine — not Alice.

"You all right?" he asked when he could catch the breath she'd knocked out of him.

Alice reached up and touched his angular face. "Are you for real?"

"I ain't no angel. Why'd you jump off the ladder like that?"

"Well, I'm quite sure I didn't do it on purpose. I was stretching to get the paper up and fell," she said indignantly.

"You reckon you could get off me?"

She rolled to one side and sat up.

He breathed like each breath was his last and stared at the ceiling.

"I expect you're here to talk to Catherine?" she asked.

"Guess I am," he said. He'd forgotten how pretty Alice was. To his notion she'd always been the prettiest of the three O'Shea girls, with her medium red hair and those grassy green eyes with yellow shot through them. He'd always liked that pert little nose sprinkled with freckles and her artistic abilities, but those things didn't make for a stable wife. Where Alice had always been rather light in the brain area, Catherine was solid and dependable. It had been said that their mother, Ella, named them for the elements. Catherine for earth; Alice for air; Bridget for water. Ella had branded them for sure because that's just the way they turned out. Catherine, responsible; Alice, air for brains; Bridget, as unstable as water.

Alice hated to be the bearer of bad news but she was the only one at home. Bridget was at the general store, putting in the weekly order for the Black Swan Café. Sadie, the girl they'd hired to help with the cleaning, had finished for the day and had gone back across the lawn to her sister's house.

8

Ira finally sat up. "So?"

"So why aren't you dead?" Alice asked.

Ira had filled out a little. He'd always looked like a strong north wind could blow him halfway around the world, but he'd put a few pounds on his lanky body. His face was still a study in angles like she remembered. His nose strong with just a hint of a bump in the middle; chin only slightly weak but a firm mouth that made up for it. His hair thick and dark brown; eyes the color of a summer sky. It had always been his eyes that had drawn her back to him before he died. She'd sketched him from every imaginable perspective and that particular book had been hidden away in her own private place. After all, he'd been Catherine's fiancé.

He finally sat up.

The Black Swan, a local small hotel known for its hospitality and good food, hadn't changed. It was still a big white two-story building with a lobby, and a symbol of a black swan inside a circle on the sign in the front yard and also painted on the front door. "It's a long story," he said.

"So tell it," she said.

"I reckon I ought to tell Catherine first, don't you? Could I bother you for a glass of water, though?"

"I'm sorry, Ira. I should have offered. Have you had your lunch? There's ham in the kitchen. I could make you a sandwich and we've got banana cream pie."

"Water will be fine. I don't have money to pay for food," he said. "I'm on my way home. Mother will have food."

Oh, dear Lord. She actually rolled her eyes but God didn't send down a band of angels to tell Ira about his parents. *He knows nothing and I'm the one who has to tell him? That's not fair, God. I could accept he was in love with Catherine, but this just ain't dang fair.*

"Come on," Alice stood up and started through the dining room into the kitchen. The hotel had been built sixteen years before, back when Huttig, Arkansas, was enduring the birthing pains of becoming a town. The sawmill was already located there and the men who worked at it wanted places to live, schools, churches — the types of things that would create a town for their wives and children. So Huttig was literally carved out of the tall pine trees. The Black Swan was one of the first hotels built in town. Patrick O'Shea had brought his wife, Ella, and three young daughters on the train from northern Arkansas, and they lived in a two-room sawmill house until they finished building the hotel. They'd done well in the

10

business until the previous fall when the great flu epidemic hit. Patrick was one of the first in Huttig to succumb to it. Ella, one of the final cases.

Ira took stock as he followed her. A huge fireplace sat on one wall, cold now in the heat of August, but always blazing in the winter with a warm fire beckoning both local folks and travelers to come and warm their hands. Comfortable sofas and chairs offered the hotel guests a place to sit and read or visit. She herded him through an archway into the dining room where tables were set with linen napkins and vases of flowers. The aromas in the kitchen made him dizzy. It had only been two days since he'd eaten. He'd gone longer than that many times.

Alice set about making a sandwich with a half-inch slab of cold ham laid between two thick pieces of homemade bread. She sliced tomatoes and cucumbers and laid them on the side. She poured a glass of water and one of sweet tea and put them on a tray.

"I said I don't have money," he told her.

"I didn't ask for any money, did I? Come on in the dining room, Ira. We're going to talk at a table while you eat. You look like a summer breeze could knock you plumb down."

"I'm obliged," he said hoarsely.

It had been a very long time since he'd drawn a chair up to a table covered with a cloth and napkins. He felt awkward as he laid the napkin on his lap before he remembered he hadn't washed his hands nor combed his hair. "I should wash up first."

She pointed at the sandwich. "You should eat first."

"Yes, ma'am." He picked up the food and fought the urge to gulp it down in four bites, forcing himself to eat slowly and drink sparingly.

"When you finish, you can tell me how you got resurrected from the dead. We got a telegram that said you were killed in action."

His hands shook as he ate. Hunger could do that and Alice wouldn't have a friend of the O'Shea family leave their kitchen still wanting. While he chewed on the last bite she went back to the kitchen and made him another sandwich and put a third of a banana pie on a dinner plate. He'd best have a full stomach for what she was about to tell him. An empty one would cause him to faint for sure and she didn't think she was big enough to catch him like he had her.

She set the food in front of him and he

12

ate. When he finished he carefully wiped his mouth with the napkin and laid it beside the plate. "I thank you for a lovely meal, Miss Alice. Now could you go get Catherine?"

"After you tell me why you aren't dead," she said.

"But I only want to tell it once and . . . Where is Catherine, anyway? Did that flu take her?" he asked.

"No, it didn't, but she's not here so tell me," Alice said.

"Where is she?"

"Okay, I'll go first since you aren't going to tell me a blessed thing until I talk. But you're not going to like it and I hate to be the bearer of all this bad news, Ira. You sure you don't want to talk awhile first?"

"Just tell me where Catherine is," he said hoarsely. He didn't want her to be dead even if he had come straight from the train station to the Black Swan before going home so he could tell her exactly how he felt.

"First, I'm going to tell you about your folks and mine. Did you hear about the flu and how many people it took?"

He blanched. "My parents?"

She moved her chair closer to his and put her arm around his shoulders. "And mine."

13

"Both of them?"

"And both of mine. Daddy was one of the first to go, then your family, and Momma was the last one we buried last spring."

"Ray and Cletus . . ." His voice was thin and on the brink of tears. Memories of his family was what brought him back from that terrifying black hole called war, and now they were gone.

"Ray and Cletus and their wives and children are dead," she said bluntly. "The flu got them all within a month of each other. You want to go to the cemetery, you can use our car or the bike out in the shed, either one."

"My whole family is gone?" he asked incredulously. It was his punishment for what he'd been about to do — tell Catherine he wasn't in love with her and break their engagement.

"I'm very sorry, Ira. We were numb when Daddy died and barely got through it when Momma went. I can't imagine hearing what I just told you."

"The house?"

"The town folks got in touch with your grandparents and sent their personal things out there by train. The house has been let out to another sawmill family who needed it," she said.

14

He had no family, no home, and no money. Ira McNewel was nothing more than a hobo. He'd clawed his way out of the black hole for nothing.

"There's more," Alice said.

He shook his head. He didn't think he could bear another word of bad news. He'd been better off dead.

"I guess I'll go on over to the mill and get my old job back," he said, prolonging any more terrible words.

"Sawmill isn't hiring. It's laid off so many people that we're afraid the town is going to be a ghost town before long. Contracts from the war projects are over so there's not as big a demand for the wood. They're still operating, but all those extra folks they hired for the war effort contracts had to be let go and they aren't taking on any more," Alice said.

It was the last straw. Ira had never cried in front of a woman before, but he couldn't control the ache deep in his soul. He laid his head on the table and great sobs shook his bony shoulders.

Alice patted his back and wept with him. At that moment she could have wrung her older sister's neck for leaving her with this mess. But then she couldn't blame Catherine. She'd gotten the telegram saying Ira

McNewel was dead and she'd simply moved on with her life. Alice had even encouraged her older sister to do so. Just because Alice never felt Ira was dead wasn't any reason for anyone else to doubt the government's word on the issue.

Finally, he wiped his face with the napkin and squared his shoulders. The news had been devastating but he was alive and a grown man. He'd proven that he was a survivor the past eighteen months and he would bear up under what Alice had just unloaded on him. How on earth he'd keep his body and soul together until he found a job was another matter. He'd kept telling himself that if he could make it home to Huttig everything would be fine. He'd work at the mill, sleep in his old room in his own bed, work through his demons, and put the whole war experience behind him.

"When the telegram came telling your folks that you were dead, the man didn't know where to take it since your folks were all gone by then. So he brought it here. Catherine took it," Alice said.

"Where is she? Did the flu take her too?"

"No, she's alive and well. She is in Galveston, Texas. It's a long story. Come on in here to the lobby so you can have a softer seat." Alice led the way again.

16

He settled into a sofa wishing that someone would yell his name and he'd awaken to find that this, like so many other times, was nothing but a nightmare.

"Okay, here goes. Right after you left, Ralph Contiello, a man from El Dorado, came down to Huttig on business and stayed here at the Black Swan. He saw Bridget and started courting her. They got married a little later, only it wasn't a good marriage. He beat her awful and when Momma took sick he told her she couldn't come home."

All the anger in Ira's heart clamped onto the man who'd beat Bridget, and he vowed he'd take care of the issue before the week was out. He'd grown up with the O'Shea sisters and none of them deserved that treatment.

Alice went on. "Bridget came anyway and was able to see Momma before she died. We buried her the next day and that evening Ralph came in here like a tornado, screaming and yelling at Bridget. Catherine was in the dining room and Bridget and I were upstairs doing some cleaning just to keep our mind off Momma's passing. Anyway, here Ralph comes tearing up the stairs telling her just what he was going to do to her for disobeying him. She had Momma's little gun in her pocket because she'd made up her mind she wasn't going back with him, and she pointed it at him. He didn't scare too easy, at least not until she pulled the trigger. It missed and landed in the woodwork beside one of the bedrooms, but it did scare him."

"What has this got to do with Catherine?" Ira asked.

Alice held up a hand. "I'm getting to it. You got to know the past before you can know the future. Anyway, Ralph left and we never heard from him again. But his family is big and important so they sent a detective down here to do an investigation. His name is Quincy Massey and lord was he persistent. He even dug up the garden and the rosebushes hunting for Ralph's body. Just couldn't get it through his thick skull we hadn't killed and buried Ralph right here on the property. Finally he gave up and figured there wasn't a dead body hiding around here. He was about to leave Huttig when he got a job at the mill, but it was really an undercover thing to uncover some men who were causing trouble. After that he went on back to Little Rock and anyway, he and Catherine met in El Dorado when she went up there on hotel business, and this is getting to be too much explaining.

18

They fell in love and she married him. They're going to live in Little Rock after they get through with a job in Galveston. Ira, she thought you were dead."

He'd figured out months ago that he didn't love Catherine but the gentlemanly thing to do was tell her face-to-face, not in a cold letter. Her heart would be broken but he owed her more than words on paper. But hearing that she'd married and went right on with her life was another blow to his pride.

"Is that all?" he finally asked.

She nodded.

"Well, I thank you again for the food. I'll be going now."

"Where are you going? You told me you didn't have money to eat. You need a job and . . ." Alice took a deep breath. She couldn't let Ira McNewel walk out of her life but she needed to talk to Bridget before she made such a big decision.

"I'll be fine, Alice. When you write to Catherine, tell her I truly wish her a happy marriage."

"I've been looking to hire someone to help with the work around here. I'll pay whatever the mill would pay you if you worked for them," she blurted out.

"I'm not a charity case. I can find work."

"Who said you were a charity case? I intend to work the dickens out of you, Ira. We need the whole place repapered and the outside painted before winter. Then we need a floor put in the basement and don't get me started on the attic. Poppa always intended to do all that but never got around to it. And we've been looking to hire someone but we didn't want just any old body since we were going to offer room and board as part of the job. We've been short on business the past few months because we're just two women in the hotel and I might as well tell you, some folks don't stay here because Bridget is expecting a baby and she divorced Ralph after he disappeared and took her maiden name back. Folks think that is a disgrace and don't want to stay here. They'll eat here but not sleep here. Anyway, if there was a man on the premises, it would be better for business. So are you going to take this job or not?"

Ira had never heard Alice say so much so fast in her life, and he'd known her since she was four years old. He'd never thought of himself as a handyman but it was a job and it paid real money. By Christmas he would have a bit of savings and could catch a train to his grandparents' farm in Grace, Mississippi. Still he hesitated. It might not be such a good idea to take his orders from Alice. Lord, she might want him to do something totally irrational, the way her mind worked.

"Dollar a day and room and board. You can start right now. I'm terrible at hanging wallpaper but Bridget is eight months pregnant and she sure can't crawl up on a ladder. I told Catherine we could run this place without her. You going to help me or make a liar out of me?"

He stuck out his hand. "It's a deal. I'll work for you until Christmas."

CHAPTER TWO

Alice could hardly believe her ears. She didn't have to spend her whole afternoon fighting twelve-foot lengths of wallpaper. She had help not with only that but painting and plowing and all those other things her father took care of while he was alive.

"Thank you, Ira. I'm grateful," she said. She didn't tell him how the touch of her hand in his during a firm handshake on the deal had unsettled her nerves.

" 'Tis me who is grateful for the job. I've got a suitcase on the porch. Reckon I could bring it in and change into old clothes before I get busy on that paper?"

"Of course. We've only got one guest right now. She's staying in the first room on the left. You can have any of the others. Take your pick," Alice said. She didn't comment on the fact that the clothing he wore was so old and tattered she couldn't imagine anything worse.

"Thank you. I'll change and get to work then."

He stood up and sucked in air so visibly that Alice half expected him to drop dead with a heart attack. "Bridget?" he whispered.

"Ira McNewel, you are dead," she said from the doorway.

"No, he's back from that place but he hasn't told us yet how he got resurrected. I did hire him to do some work around here, and he's agreed to stay until Christmas, Bridget," Alice explained.

"That's good. I'm glad you aren't dead. We need help. I'm going to prop my feet up until suppertime. They are swelling but the doctor says that's normal for this time of the ordeal. It's good to have you back, Ira. I expect Alice explained about Catherine?"

"She did." Ira couldn't take his eyes from the bulge under Bridget's flowing overalls. It looked as if she carried a litter under there instead of one baby, but then he hadn't seen many pregnant women as far along as she was. Most women still hid themselves away as much as possible those last few weeks.

"I'm right sorry about that. If she'd have known you were alive things might've been different, but they aren't, so it is what it is and we'll be glad for your help. Make yourself at home in the kitchen and pick a room. We're still feeding half of southern Arkansas even if we aren't bedding them down. Looks like Alice lost another strip of paper." She nodded toward the wrinkled mess on the floor.

"Yes, ma'am, she did, and then she fell on me. Knocked the breath right out of me," Ira said.

"That wasn't very hospitable of her, now was it?" Bridget smiled.

Even big with child, Bridget was a lovely woman. She had strawberry blond hair, light aqua-colored eyes, and a perfect little round face that caused a man to immediately go into a protective mode. She was not nearly as breathtaking as Alice but still a pretty young woman. Her ex-husband must have had cow chips for brains if he didn't appreciate her beauty, and he was a complete idiot for ever hitting her.

"I'll change and get to work then. Alice already fed me sandwiches and pie, for which I am grateful. I'd almost work for food but I'll be glad to make a few dollars. I told Alice I'd work until Christmas."

"That will be very good. Maybe we'll entice you to stay longer but we'll take all the help we can get. At least by then, I'll be back to normal," Bridget said as she opened the door at the back of the lobby into their private living quarters.

Ira carried his tattered suitcase up the stairs to the first room on the right at the top of the steps. The accommodations were downright luxurious in comparison to what he'd had even before the war; they were even beyond that compared to the past months he'd spent in the hospital and then the barracks. A full-size bed with crisp white sheets and a patchwork quilt was pushed up against the wall on the left. An oak dresser with a mirror and three wide, deep drawers matched the bedstead. The rocking chair setting beside an open window with a breeze blowing the crisp white curtains beckoned him to come and sit a spell, but he couldn't. Ira had paper to hang and a real bath to take afterward, then he had supper to eat right there in the Black Swan restaurant.

He changed from khaki-colored trousers and a blue chambray work shirt, both with patches in various places, into a pair of faded, threadbare overalls and a short-sleeved shirt that had been checkered blue-and-white at one time. He only had the one pair of shoes and the soles were paper thin. Maybe he'd buy new shoes with his first paycheck from the hotel and a new selection of clothes, but he'd be very careful with his money because as soon as winter set in he was heading for Mississippi to what was left of his blood kin.

Alice wadded up the strip of paper she'd been hanging when she fell off the ladder. She hated to waste it but it had stuck to itself and was all wrinkled. Lord, who would have thought the day would turn out like it had, and it wasn't finished. After supper she really should write Catherine a long letter and tell her what had happened. Maybe by then she'd have the story of why the government had said Ira was dead and could tell Catherine all about that too. She put the ball of paper in the tall trash can she'd hauled in from the back porch, along with the rest of the scraps. She took time to make a dash through her bedroom in the O'Shea's private quarters. The mirror above her dresser made her gasp in horror. She'd braided her red hair that morning and wrapped the ropes around her head like a crown. They'd fallen into loops hanging on her shoulders. Her cheeks were rosy and her freckles popped out like ugly blotches. Her blouse had globs of dried flour and water paste on the collar and her overalls were so faded and worn they belonged in a rag bag.

And Ira had seen her looking like that!

She hurriedly repaired the damage to her

hair, whipping the braids down to undo them and twist her hair into a French roll at the back of her head. Then she used a little of Bridget's loose face powder to cover her freckles. There wasn't one reason to change her clothing since she'd planned to help Ira with the paper-hanging job, but to look so shabby didn't sit well with her. Not when it came to Ira.

Ira was no stranger to wallpaper but he'd never dealt with it in twelve-foot lengths. The sawmill house where he'd been raised had eight-foot ceilings, making the job much, much easier. He had unrolled a length and had it ready to cut when Alice returned.

"I need a square," he said.

"What's that?"

"It's a metal tool that looks like a square. Two-sided. How have you been cutting this paper?"

"With scissors. It doesn't matter if the edges are perfect. I've got a six-inch border to go around the top when I'm finished," she said.

"It matters to me and it makes the job go faster. I need a square. Did your father keep his tools out in the shed with your bicycle?"

"You are welcome to go look," she said testily. Men! God surely had a sense of humor when he made them, and even a greater one when he made women to be attracted to them.

She didn't offer him the short route through their private quarters but rather let him go out the front door, around the hotel, and to the shed at the far back corner of the yard, beyond the garden. If he wanted a square that badly, he could find it. The scissors worked perfectly fine. The part she needed help with was simply manhandling a long length without dropping it.

"Found it," he said cheerfully when he returned in less than five minutes.

He measured the length of the wall, added two inches, and then unrolled the paper across the floor. He laid the square on the line he'd drawn at precisely twelve feet two inches, making sure the side against the paper was exactly even with the edge. Then he gave it a rip along the metal edge and it tore perfectly on the pencil line.

"Now I'll use this one to get a perfect match on the next one, like this," he mumbled as he worked.

He made sure the edges of the daisies on the second piece lined up with the first and muttered something about losing six inches to get a good match, but it was important. After he made the cut and tear, he gently turned the first piece over. "Now you can paste this one while I cut and number the next."

It was a good method but it irked Alice to have to admit it. She'd watched her mother and Catherine put up new paper a couple of times in the sixteen years they'd owned the Black Swan. They'd never done it that way and it always looked good, so why did Ira have to be such a perfectionist?

Oh, stop it right now. He's doing the job right rather than half-witted. It doesn't matter how it gets done. You hired him so let him work.

Using a four-inch brush, she painted paste on the backside of the paper as evenly as possible while he cut four more pieces and numbered them according to the way they'd go up on the wall.

"Where's your plumb line mark?" he asked.

She cocked her head to one side and looked at him quizzically.

"You know the mark you make so you know where to start?"

"I just used the edge of the paper already up there," she said.

He rolled his eyes.

"Don't you roll those eyes at me, Ira Mc-Newel. I don't know anything about plums unless you're talking about jelly making. If you want to put one up there, then get after it, but don't look at me like I'm stupid."

He almost told her that she wasn't one hundred percent smart and never had been, but kept his mouth shut. Even if Catherine wasn't around to take up for her dim-witted sister, it would be rude of him to say such a thing. Besides, Alice had hired him and he owed her a little respect. And Lord only knew how badly he needed the money she'd promised him.

"I'll look in the shed for the plumb line," he said.

"Plum line, orange line, apple line. What difference does it make anyway? Momma and Catherine did it right so why can't I just use their work to go by? God Almighty, who would have thought Daddy did so much around here?" she mumbled as she turned over the next piece and dipped her brush in the glue mixture.

"Don't do that!" Ira shouted from the door. "It will dry before we can get it up. Only paste one strip at a time."

She jumped and glared at him. "Don't yell at me. And why do you doubt the work my sister and my mother did? Right there, you can see the line of the old paper. Why don't you just use that for a guide?"

Ira inhaled deeply. "Because the hotel

could have settled since this paper was hung and if it did even a quarter of an inch by the time you get around the whole room with each piece off just slightly, your daisies would be layin' down rather than standin' up."

She set her jaw in a firm line. "Don't talk down to me."

"I don't mean to. I was just explaining. Could we get this done now or are you going to fight me on every turn?"

"I'm not stupid or dumb, Ira. Don't treat me like a child. I'm twenty years old and I know what people in Huttig say about me, but I do have sense. So get on with it," she said.

Alice O'Shea not dumb? Now that was a novel idea. She'd been dancing to the beat of a different jazz band since the day she was born and didn't give a tin hoot who knew or cared. Being twenty years old didn't change a blessed thing.

He climbed the ladder to the top rung and let the plumb line fall to the floor. "Would you please hold that steady?" he asked.

She did as he asked and he popped the string. A thin blue chalk line showed the old paper was indeed slightly off plumb. A memory of someone saying that about Alice rose to the top of her mind.

So that's what it meant. I never knew but now I do. It means I'm not lined up with society's idea of straight up and down. Well, who cares? I never have . . . until now. I don't want Ira to think I'm off plumb. I want him to see me as a woman instead of Catherine's odd sister. And Lord only knows why.

"Okay, now we'll fold the piece you've glued very gently so we don't make a seam. We'll leave a foot at the top for a starter and keep the edge of the paper on the plumb line," he talked as he came down from the ladder and worked. Maybe if he explained it slowly and carefully she'd understand.

He carried the folded strip to the top of the ladder, set it against the edge of the ceiling, and using a smoothing cloth began to work the paper as she held the bottom part. When he had that area done he peeled back the part that had been folded up on itself and let it fall.

"Grab an area and hold it against the wall so we don't lose the top." He barked orders and she followed them. "I've got to make sure it stays on the line, but keep it from stretching or else the seams won't be perfect."

"Who'd have thought there was so much to such a simple job?" she mumbled.

"What was that?"

"Nothing. Not a single thing. You've still got bubbles under the paper right there."

"They don't matter. They're just little ones. You got a straight pin ready?"

"What for?"

"This big one. I need to poke a hole in it so the air will come out that way rather than having to push it to the side and stretch the paper," he said.

She stopped long enough to find a pin in Bridget's sewing basket beside the fireplace. It took a full fifteen minutes before he was satisfied with the way the paper and bubbles looked before he gave her permission to glue up the piece with a big number two written on the back.

When they reached the corner he deftly split the paper with a razor blade she had rustled up from the kitchen; he overlaid the pattern so expertly she couldn't even see where the cut had been made. She was very glad she'd hired him by the time they got to the fireplace and had to work around it and the windows.

Bridget came out when they were half finished. "Okay, you two, push it back and let's get ready for supper."

"Is it that time already?" Ira smiled.

Alice bristled. How dare he smile at

Bridget. The woman was pregnant for goodness' sake and barely over the disappearance of her husband. But then, no one except the three sisters actually knew about the death. Everyone else around Huttig figured he'd run off with another woman or else gotten himself killed by an irate husband. Ralph had been the kind who didn't play by the rules. If he wanted it, it was already his, whether it was illegal or immoral. So it had been easy to tell the story that he'd simply disappeared. Only the three sisters knew how and where he'd disappeared to, and that he would never be coming back again.

"Time gets away from us when we're busy," Bridget said. "Alice, I told Sadie to start coming back in the evenings for a couple of hours to help us in the kitchen. Should have mentioned it to you this morning, but I just flat forgot."

"Hello," Sadie said from the front door.

Bridget motioned to the young woman. "Come on back. I'll show you what I want you to do. I'm not ashamed of the way I look but it seems to embarrass folks. So starting tonight I'm staying in the kitchen and you are going to serve."

She stopped dead in the middle of the room and pointed at Ira. "I'm Sadie. My

34

sister, Lizzy, lives next door over there. And you are?"

"I'm Ira McNewel, the new handyman. Pleased to meet you, Sadie."

Sadie was a pretty, dark-haired woman of eighteen with big brown eyes and fluttering eyelashes. She wore a crisp, freshly ironed blue dress with a white lace collar and her black hair was cut in one of those new fashionable styles called a bob. She knew how to flirt and Ira didn't stand a chance if she set her cap for him. Alice felt her heart drop to the floor.

"We can finish this room tomorrow. Ira, go on up and get cleaned up for supper," Alice said quickly.

"I reckon I could go ahead and get the rest of the pieces cut while you ladies get things ready. I'll still have time for a bath and clean-up after that." He went back to work.

Alice threw up her hands. She'd hired him. She was the boss, so why didn't he listen to orders instead of doing things the way he wanted? This was never going to work. She'd pay him at the end of the week and send him on his way.

She followed Bridget and Sadie into the kitchen, only to have to listen to Sadie go on and on about how good-looking the new

35

handyman was and how she wouldn't mind walking around town with him any night after work.

Alice went to work slicing ham and setting the pans of candied sweet potatoes in the oven to warm. "I'm surprised you'd think someone that tall and gangly is good-looking."

"Oh, there's lots of men now that the war is over, but not many have a job. That's where the difference is, Alice. You don't have to be worrying about a man with a job. You and Bridget own a hotel and have money, but if I'm going to find a husband, I have to look for one who can support me. And Ira, bless his heart, might not be the best-looking one I've seen around Huttig these past couple of months, but he does have a job."

"What about falling in love with him?"

"Oh, that's nice, but it's not the be all and end all of a marriage is it, Bridget?"

"Don't be asking me anything about marriage. I think it's a sorry state of affairs any way you look at it. Way I see it is, if you want to marry a man it should be written at the courthouse in pencil and the bride has two months to erase it before it's written in ink," Bridget said.

"Why two months?" Sadie asked.

"If she doesn't know in that length of time that she's married a monster, she deserves to keep him," Bridget said.

Alice just listened and wondered if she'd made the biggest mistake of her life in hiring Ira. Maybe she should have loaned him the money to go on to Mississippi and kept her dreams to herself.

CHAPTER THREE

The night was warm with summer breezes fluffing the fronds of the Boston ferns hanging in baskets on the porch. The fragrance of roses and lilacs wafted from one side of the porch to the other. Crickets and tree frogs joined together in an attempt at country opera. The day's work was finished and it was time to sit outside and enjoy the evening.

Ira had one leg stretched out so his foot rested on the ground, the other propped up to the second porch step and his back resting against the newel. Even with the devastating news of his family bearing down on his mind, he was home and glad he hadn't found out about them in a letter when he was thousands of miles away.

Bridget opened the door and carried her stitching bag out to the porch. She nodded at Ira but neither of them actually said a word, both in their own world of thought and not really caring what the other was pondering.

At the beginning of her pregnancy Bridget had knit several baby items but lately she'd gone to hemming flannel nappies. There were those folks who said the baby she was carrying didn't belong to Ralph Contiello, that if it did she wouldn't have taken back her maiden name with the divorce. Some speculated that the whole reason Ralph was so mean to her was because he knew she was cheating on him. Bridget didn't care what they thought or said. She knew the truth. Ralph had used her as an outlet for his anger the whole year they were married; the baby was his although she'd be happy to have it belong to a railroad hobo; and she never had cheated and would never marry again.

Normally Alice would be sitting on the far end of the porch so she could sketch by the light coming from the lobby window. But that night she drew her rocking chair up close to Bridget when she came out to the porch for a breath of fresh air.

"So you were going to tell us why you aren't dead?"

"It's a long story," Ira answered. He'd never put the whole thing into words and didn't know if he was even able to do so.

"We're listening and we're interested," Alice said.

"Okay, I'll try." It was the least he could do when they'd given him a place to stay, a job, and meals. "But only once. I'm not telling it but this one time and that's all. It's the past and I don't want to remember."

"You don't have to tell us anything," Bridget said.

Alice shook her head. "I want to hear it."

"It was late May last year. The Battle of Cantigny. I wasn't even supposed to be there but there had been a few problems with some equipment so they sent me and two other men who were good with the tracked vehicles to do some maintenance. The troops only gained a mile that day but it was a big battle. Fifty miles on over there was another bigger battle going on. Anyway, the French sent in air support and flame throwers and when the dust and smoke settled they'd captured the German observation point. The French sent in a dozen tanks ahead of the troops. I was a mechanic and should have brought up the rear, only coming into the town after it was secured. In a battle things don't always play out the way they're supposed to," he said. He picked up a glass of cold tea he'd brought with him from the kitchen and drank heavily, almost tasting the dirt from that day more than a year before.

"More than a thousand men lost their lives that day. I was told to grab a gun from one of the fallen soldiers and fight, so I did. Thirty minutes later I was flat on my back with a bullet in my bad leg, a grazed rip in my scalp, and everything went black. They loaded up the wounded and dead and I fell among the latter. My dog tags had disappeared so no one even knew who I was. The only identification they could find was the rifle and one of the living said it belonged to his buddy, Sam Willows, from Tennessee. He never got around to actually looking at me or they'd have known I wasn't Sam, so I was sent to the place set up for the dead bodies. They told me later that when they were about to put me in a wooden box to be shipped back home for burial, I moved a finger."

Alice shivered.

Bridget declared she'd heard enough and if Alice wanted to know the rest she could hear it alone. She took her sewing basket into the house.

Ira waited until the door was closed before he continued. "From what I pieced together later, one of the other mechanics found my dog tags in the mud and blood and gore left behind and there was a body close by. It had been shot and run over with a tank and had no tags but it was wearing a uniform something like mine, so they decided that's who it was. You've got to understand what a mess it all was. That they ever got any of the bodies home for proper funerals was a miracle."

"So they found out you were alive. What next?" Alice asked.

"I was taken to a hospital but that one had no room and I was shifted to another and still another. Somehow I was put on a plane with another man who wasn't expected to live either and wound up in Russia, in a town by the name of Tsarskoe Selo, in a place where they figured they'd have to amputate my leg if I survived the head wound, which was infected by that time. There was a very kind doctor there who had some knowledge of such infection and I became his experiment. I don't know about these things really because when I woke up, it was three months later and I was still Sam."

"Amnesia?" Alice asked.

"I don't think so. Not like a body thinks when he hears that word anyway. It was a strange thing. I knew my name wasn't Sam. I knew it was Ira but I couldn't tell them.

So I drifted in between reality and dreams for weeks. I fell in love with my nurse, which the doctor said later wasn't uncommon, especially with the injuries I had. I remembered that I was engaged to Catherine and found out the nurse was married the same day. I promised myself that if I ever got out of that place, I would tell Catherine the truth. If I could love someone else then I didn't love her with the proper kind of love to marry her. I was relieved when I found out she'd married someone else. I'm glad she didn't mourn my death and forget how to live. I should have known she was stronger than that."

"Yes, you should have. Catherine is the earth. She's always been strong and always will be." Alice wished she'd been the one named for the earth instead of air. Her mother could have given her a better name if it was going to govern her whole attitude and life.

After another drink of tea, Ira went on. "So the doctor was treating my leg at the same time, even though he figured it was a lost cause. He gave me as much pain medication as he could to keep the pain itself from killing me, and I suppose that's what kept me out of my mind longer than it should have. Anyway, at one point they

43

determined I'd gotten an abscess on my brain and they took me to the surgery room. He shaved my head but I didn't ask how they took care of it. He told me later they'd drained it, so I suppose they drilled a hole through my skull. At that point, I scarcely knew who I was or knew the difference between life and death.

"By the time they'd weaned me off the pain stuff, months had elapsed. I was the experiment that worked and my leg wasn't all that much worse than it had been when I enlisted. It's a little stiffer now but I can live with that better than living with no leg. I remember the day the nurse brought my dinner and I told her I was not Sam. I was Ira McNewell of Huttig, Arkansas. She patted my arm and said that was okay, I could be whoever I wanted to be.

"When the doctor came in later, I told him the same thing. It took a week before anyone would believe me. By then I understood that everyone in my family had been told I was dead. Seemed the only fitting thing to do was come home and show them. Mother didn't trust the government anyway. If they said I was dead and then said I wasn't dead, she wouldn't have believed it until I was standing in front of her. So I didn't write. I just healed. By the time that was done the war was over and they shipped me to New York, gave me enough money for train fare back home, and you know the rest."

"Thank you for telling me," Alice said.

"Thank you for listening," he said. "I didn't know what a weight it would lift from my shoulders to just tell it all and get it out of my system."

Alice nodded. He hadn't told it all any more than they'd told the whole story of Ralph's disappearance last spring. She and her sisters had made a pact not to tell the whole story, and she never would, but she understood the concept of telling the truth without telling it all. Maybe he couldn't go into minute detail of those months when he thought he'd die or come home an amputee without it tearing at his soul so he just kept it simple and skimmed the surface of the real feelings. Alice would bet he had nightmares about the demons, because she still did about Ralph.

She dreamed often of the blank look in Ralph's open dead eyes when he tumbled down the stairs and broke his fool neck. She wasn't sorry he was dead. She wasn't sorry they took care of his body and kept Bridget out of prison. But she still had nightmares and that was nothing compared to what Ira had endured.

As if he could read her mind, he asked, "So tell me, what do you think really happened to Bridget's husband?"

She blushed hot enough that she was sure they could light a candle by holding the wick to her cheeks. "I hope he's pushin' up daisies somewhere and never bothers her again."

"You said they are divorced. Bet that was a hard thing to get done," he said.

"Catherine took care of most of it. I've got a feeling her new husband, Quincy, helped out in some way by getting it done so fast, but he'd never admit to it. He was determined to find Ralph, dead or alive. Guess it's the only time he failed at his job."

"Tell me about Quincy," Ira said.

"He's taller than she is, got dark hair and eyes. Nice-looking man and they make a pretty couple. Folks around here think he's been married before. I told you about him being on a detective job at the mill — well, they sent him a wife to make it look more real. Her name was Elizabeth and we all took to her, even Catherine. Anyway it turned out that she was actually engaged to another detective and in real life was Quincy's cousin. She sent a letter to us after she left saying that her first husband, whom

46

she'd married before Quincy, was killed in the war, but they'd made this mistake and he'd come home so she had her marriage to Quincy annulled. So everyone in town believes that story. It's not true but she wanted things to be right for Catherine. At least that's what I think. Be nice if you didn't tell anyone else," Alice said.

"I'm the real-life thing."

"Real-life what?" The other hotel guest, Dottie, came from around the end of the house and pulled up a rocking chair. A young lady making a trip from somewhere in Missouri to New Orleans, she had stopped off for a couple of days to visit her mother's cousin, Mabel Matthis, who lived next door to the hotel.

"Real-life soldier who came home after he was declared dead by the government," Alice said.

Ira was shocked that Alice could answer so quickly and without thinking about it. She wasn't as slow as folks had said all those years. Matter of fact, he'd forgotten all about the rumors as they talked that evening.

Dottie shivered. "Well, I don't want to hear any of those horror stories. I'm just glad it's over. Too many of my acquaintances had to go and too many didn't come back.

47

We had a lovely bridge game at Mabel's this evening. I really should have stayed with her, I suppose. But one never knows. She and Momma never got along and Momma thought it best I stay in a hotel. Momma isn't as outgoing as Mabel. I'd say I inherited more of Mabel's qualities than Momma's. Now tell me, Mr. Ira McNewell, what brought you to Huttig?"

"It's home, or was. My family is all gone now but it's where I was raised the past sixteen years and I didn't know until this morning that the flu got them, so I simply came home."

"The night is so pretty. Since you are from this place maybe you'd like to walk with me and show me the sights," Dottie flirted.

Alice envisioned strangling her until she was blue and giving Ralph some company for all eternity. No doubt Dottie wouldn't even get her wings and halo checked out before Ralph would be chasing her all over hell, the kind of rogue he'd been, and Alice danged sure didn't see him changing a bit even for a passport out of hell and into heaven.

Ira shook his head and stood up. His limp was more pronounced than it had been because he'd been sitting so long. He picked up his glass and headed inside. "I'd be

48

delighted but I've had a long day and tomorrow morning will start early. Miss Alice has been kind enough to give me a job here at the Black Swan and I'll be up at the crack of dawn to work. I think I'll turn in now. You ladies have a nice visit."

Dottie was a nice-looking woman. She had dark brown hair with just a hint of curl that sent errant strands to tickle the sides of her face, light brown eyes, and a ready smile. A little on the heavy side and giggled entirely too much but it wouldn't have hurt him to take a walk with her. Tomorrow evening after work, he would go to the cemetery and tell his family good-bye and talk to his mother. It didn't seem right to go out walking with a woman until he'd paid his proper respects. At least that's what Ira told himself as he carried the teacup back to the kitchen.

He went to his room and stripped out of his better clothes, stretched out on the featherbed in only his underwear, and enjoyed the breeze blowing in the open window. The sheets were fresh and pillowcases crisp. He thought about everything that he'd learned that day and tears rolled down the sides of his face, leaving wet spots on the pillows.

Dottie struggled trying to find a topic to carry on a conversation with Alice. It seemed pointless since Mabel had filled her in on the O'Shea girls and their odd ways but the woman was sitting right there and she had to say something or appear rude. Perhaps she should bring up the smell of the roses. That shouldn't be too hard to discuss with someone who was severely lacking in the intelligence area.

According to Mabel, all three of the sisters were strange. The oldest had married a detective who'd been jilted by his wife when her first husband came home from the war. Bridget married well then divorced her husband — now that alone was a disgrace. Women didn't do such things in 1919 in the big cities, much less in little backwoods places like Huttig. Then she'd taken her maiden name back when she knew she was having a child. Alice was the worst one of the trio. She was a strange bird, sketching and painting lovely scenes, but not totally right in the mind.

"So tell me about Ira. Mabel told me he was declared dead and was engaged to your sister when he left for the war," Dottie blurted out, not knowing where the words came from since she'd intended to ask about the roses.

"That's about it," Alice said. If Dottie had inherited everything from Mabel then she'd

50

be one of the biggest gossips this side of the Atlantic Ocean.

"Oh, come on, you know more. I know you do. He was talking to you all serious when I came up on the porch. Ira looks like a likely prospect for a husband. Mabel vouches for him. Says he's hardworking and he'll be all vulnerable since his heart is broken about your older sister up and marrying another man instead of waiting for Ira to come home. That and the fact the flu wiped out his whole family." She might be talking to a blank wall but then she might find out something useful. Tomorrow the dim-witted O'Shea sister wouldn't even remember the conversation so she might as well get as much as she could from her.

"He was dead so Catherine merely went on with life. Had Ira been dead, he would've wanted her to do that. He doesn't blame her one bit for what she did. Are you looking for a husband? Aren't there any men up in Missouri? Didn't they go to the war and coming home in droves like they are here looking for work?"

"Of course, but there's no one there who interests me. It's my goal to find a husband before I go home. Ira isn't hard on the eyes and he's got a job. We could live right here at the hotel and maybe I could work here

51

too. I know Mabel thinks it's a den of iniquity but I could bring some honor back to it."

Alice almost laughed. "Good luck. I'm going to bed now. Doesn't your train leave early tomorrow?"

"It does but I've decided to stay on a week. Tomorrow I'll be moving over to Mabel's house. She's been so gracious as to offer me her spare bedroom for as long as I need it. She never had a daughter and she says she'll love having one. If things go well, I might just find a home right here in Huttig and not go on to New Orleans."

"I'm sure Bridget will have your bill figured by the time you are ready to leave. Good night, Dottie."

Alice escaped into the house and to her bedroom. Bridget was sitting in the middle of her bed, cross-legged and still hemming nappies. The room was enormous and held three full-size beds, three dressers with mirrors, three rocking chairs, and three wardrobes. Their mother had liked the idea of them all growing up together in one room, telling secrets, discussing the day, drawing closer and closer together. Her strategy had worked very well, until Catherine left. Now the empty bed gave the big room a rather lonely aura.

Alice took off her dress and slipped into a cotton nightgown and stretched out on her bed. She laced her hands behind her head and stared at the ceiling. She'd made the biggest mistake of her life. Poor old Ira was going to be attacked worse than that battle he'd talked about: Sadie on one side of the hotel and looking for a husband with a job; Dottie on the other, looking for a husband so she could live near her newfound relative.

Alice would have to keep her eyes wide open and ears strained to keep him away from the altar. She owed him that much for keeping him in Huttig.

CHAPTER FOUR

Big black clouds drifted in from the southwest, bringing lightning and thunder with
them. Alice could smell the imminent rain
with every gust of southerly wind but she
didn't rush back home to the hotel. It
wasn't a cold day and the storm twisted
right around Huttig; if it did rain it would
be warm, not cold. Alice was neither salt
nor sugar and a little water wouldn't melt
her. She parked her bicycle beside her
mother's gravesite and sat down on the
grass in front of the tombstone. She pulled
weeds from around clumps of yellow daisies,
her mother's favorite flower.

"Momma, Ira ain't dead. He's come back
to Huttig and I hired him because I want
him to be around so I can see if this feeling
I've had since I was ten years old is real.
Only thing is there's two smart women out
to catch him and he's only been here since
yesterday. He's a hard worker and a hearty

eater and he makes me so mad I could wring his neck most of the time, tellin' me what to do and how to do it. I let people think I wasn't all right in the head all these years so I could go about my business and do what I wanted. Now I'm afraid that wasn't as smart as I thought."

No voices whispered in her ear. No foggy ghosts stirred around her. She'd begun to think her mother's spirit wasn't even listening when she looked up and saw Ira heading toward his family's burial plot. She tried to make herself smaller and hide behind the tombstone, but it didn't work. He waved just before he kneeled down and placed a hand on the granite stone where both his parents' names were engraved.

She could see his lips moving and he wiped away tears more than once but when he stood up his back was straight and his head held high. By the time he reached the end of the cemetery where her parents, Patrick and Ella, were buried, she was on her feet standing beside her bicycle.

"Your folks were good people. I'm sorry they are gone, Alice."

"So were yours and I'm sorry for your loss, Ira."

"This is a bit strange. It's like they've just gone away and they'll be back. Kind of like

55

me going to the war and coming home. In my mind, they aren't really dead."

"I can sure see why it would feel that way. I saw Daddy and Momma both in their caskets and still I expect to turn around and see Momma in the kitchen or Daddy at the register at the front desk."

"Reckon we'd better get on back to work on that papering business," he said.

"I suppose." She was angry with herself for riding the bicycle instead of driving the car. Now she'd have to ride it home and he'd have to walk. She couldn't ask him to walk beside her while she pushed it or there'd be gossip.

"You ever rode on the handlebars?" he asked with a wicked gleam in his eye.

"Couple of times when me and Catherine were younger," Alice said.

"We could get the work started a lot faster if I pedaled and you rode," he suggested.

She nodded and waited for him to get situated before she hopped up on the narrow bars and shifted her weight evenly along them. Her fingers touched his and she hoped the heat didn't fry them fast to the handlebars. She'd had a crush on Ira McNewel since she was ten and he was fifteen, but she'd never thought the mere feel of his calloused hand could cause such sensations.

It had to be the electricity in the air, not the actual physical touch. Lightning zigzagged in front of them and a great clap of thunder made Alice duck her head to keep it from knocking her flat off the front of the bike.

"Sit still," he said.

"Make the thunder stop."

"I can't work miracles," he yelled above the next rumble.

He tried to control his thoughts. Alice was Catherine's younger sister and she'd always been around, but when her hand brushed against his, there had been something there he'd never experienced before. He immediately wondered what it would be like to kiss her — and that was just plain wrong. He would never take advantage of a woman without all her senses and everyone knew Alice was simple.

"My hind end is numb," she protested.

He couldn't help but laugh. There was proof positive that he should put a screeching halt to any physical attraction to the woman. No self-respecting lady would say something like that to a man. Only a child who hadn't been trained properly would mention her hind end in mixed company.

"You think it's so funny, next time you can sit on the bars and I'll pedal."

"I'd like to see that. You ain't big enough

to push both our weights," he retorted.

"Honey, as skinny as you are I could carry you and run faster than you are pedaling. If you don't hurry up we're going to get soaked."

Those were fighting words. No woman was going to make fun of him like that, simple or not. He pushed harder on the pedal and soon they were flying down the dirt road. Alice's hair came loose from the pins and flew behind her, reaching out to tickle Ira's nose. She held on until her hands cramped but something wild inside her loved the speed and passion of the ride.

He started to slow down a few hundred feet from the hotel but was still traveling too fast when the front wheel found the gopher hole. Alice flew through the air like a rag doll with Ira right behind her. How on earth she landed on top of him was a complete mystery. He gasped to fill his lungs with fresh air since it had all been knocked out completely when she landed smack on top of him. Her red hair covered his face and he could feel her heart racing in perfect time with his.

"Is this jumping on me going to be a daily thing?" he asked finally.

"You threw me off the bicycle. I did not jump on you." She rolled over, pushed her hair back, and looked up into the eyes of her neighbor and Dottie.

"Well, I do declare," Mabel snapped.

"Mornin' Mabel. Did you come to help Dottie?" Alice panted.

"You O'Shea women are too wild for my cousin to be living in this hotel. I swear your sisters both have ruined reputations and it looks like you might be joining them the way you are acting, Alice O'Shea. Your mother would be mortified at the way you are carryin' on. Ira, you'd do well to stay somewhere else if you ever expect to find a decent woman."

Dottie shoved her nose a little higher in the air and sniffed loudly. "I should say so. The Commercial has available rooms you could live in. Why are you staying here?"

Ira sat up. "That's none of your business, Miss Dottie or Miz Mabel. But I'll tell you anyway. Alice has been kind enough to hire me for the next few months and give me room and board in the deal. I'd be crazy to spend my money on a room when I've got one free right here."

"Be careful, Ira McNewel. Nothing is free and you'll pay for that room with your reputation. The McNewels had a fine name in Huttig. Your mother was beyond reproach, a fine Christian woman. You are marring that name keeping company with a . . ."

Ira's eyes narrowed and his heavy brows knit into a sold line. "A what?"

"A simpleton who has no morals," Mabel said.

"That will be enough," Ira said.

"It's all right." Alice touched his arm and the shock glued her tongue to the roof of her mouth. Was it because she was a simpleton like Mabel said that he affected her so much or was it the leftovers of a childish crush?

"No, it's not. Mabel you owe Alice an apology. That was rude and ugly. I'm ashamed that you'd say such a thing about her," Ira said.

"I don't owe these alley cats anything, and if you are wise you'll get out of here while the gettin's good. Come on, Dottie. Thank God you are staying with me from now on. This place isn't fittin' for anyone."

"We just fell off the bike," Alice whispered.

Ira righted himself and extended his hand to help her. "Don't let them worry you."

"Thank you for taking up for me." She wasn't even amazed at the sensation that time she was so in shock from the harsh words Mabel had spewed out like poison.

"Hey, you are welcome. After all, you are

almost my little sister. I'd take up for my own sister if I'd had one and I will for you, Alice," he said.

She felt even more deflated at that comment than she had when Mabel looked at her like something she'd tracked in from the hog lot. His sister! So that's the way he felt. There had been nothing of the sparks on his end, only on hers.

She wiped her hand on the seat of her overalls and marched toward the house. "We've got work to do. We might as well get at it."

"Ira, could I talk to you a minute?" Dottie said from the other side of Mabel's fence.

Alice stopped midstep and glared at the woman.

"Go on in the hotel. I'm not talking to you. I don't care if you do offer me a job in your hotel, I wouldn't take it. Mabel and I will not even be over there to eat again and we plan to tell everyone we know about you O'Sheas." She raised her voice slightly.

Alice had had all she could stand for one day. She pivoted and marched across the yard and promptly slapped Dottie's face. "Don't you talk about my sisters. They are fine women and I won't have it. And don't you ever presume that you can tell me what to do."

"What are you going to do about this idiot hitting me?" Dottie turned to Ira.

"Nothing," he said.

Dottie held her red cheek and glared at them. "Then you aren't the man I thought you were. Don't come around begging me to let you court me."

"I don't reckon that was ever on my mind," Ira said.

"You are both horrible," Dottie huffed as she trotted across the yard and into Mabel's house.

"Okay, now that we've got that settled, I guess us horrible folks better get inside and go to work. Might be that we're doin' it all in vain," Ira said.

"I doubt we'll lose much business on Mabel's word. Everyone knows its worth about as much as a maggot," Alice said.

"A maggot?" He followed her into the hotel lobby just as the sky opened up and the first big drops of rain pelted down.

"That's the worst thing I could think of right then. I'll paste up the next section. We're on number eight aren't we?" She set to work but couldn't get the spiteful words out of her mind. Sure, there had been talk when Bridget came home; when Ralph disappeared; when Catherine married Quincy. But why was Mabel so mad at her for nothing more than riding home on the handlebars of a bicycle? It just didn't make sense.

Ira cut two more sections of paper before she got the homemade glue on the backside of number eight, then they worked together to hang it. She'd remembered every step he told her the day before and had even learned to roll and line the freshly cut pieces in the order they would need them. Already, after a single day, he knew for a fact what he'd suspected since they were both children: Alice O'Shea was most certainly not simpleminded. She simply did not give a hoot what people thought of her.

Sadie arrived at midmorning with an umbrella over her head. She held the door open with her foot and shook the umbrella outside before closing it and placing it in the crock stand to the left of the door. She waved at Alice, smiled at Ira, and went straight to the kitchen where Bridget was already at work. Her shy little smile was enough to set Alice's teeth on edge, but at least Sadie hadn't berated him for being in the same room with Alice.

"Dinner smells good," Ira said finally.

"Tuesday is pot roast. Bridget and I put them in the ovens this morning right after breakfast. We made the pound cake yesterday for dessert," Alice said, glad to have anything to talk about on neutral ground.

"I thought Tuesday was chocolate pie day. I had the menu memorized and thought about it often when I was gone."

"It is. I made the crust this morning and Bridget made the filling. She'll get the meringue beat up and pop them in the oven just before the dinner crowd arrives so they'll be fresh. We offer two desserts."

"You've got this down to an art, don't you?"

"Pretty much. Kind of like you having this paper business down to an art," she said.

"Ah, this ain't no art. Momma just made me help because I was so tall I could reach the ceiling without having to keep getting up and down on a chair so I learned it early on." He climbed up the ladder and stuck the top of the paper in the right spot and began to work it downward, using the trusty straight pin to make an escape hole for the big bubbles.

"That's the way we feel about cooking. We serve the same thing all the time so we know exactly what to do each day. I bet you did get hungry for home cooking, didn't you?" She helped as long as she was needed then pasted up another strip.

He took it from her hands, careful not to let his fingertips touch hers. It just didn't seem right to have feelings for Alice. Not when she'd have been his younger sister had he married Catherine. Besides, even if he did, which he wasn't about to admit to, she was a wealthy hotel owner and he didn't have two copper pennies to rub together in his pockets.

Sadie poked her head into the room. "Bridget wants to know if you two want a midmorning snack? She says she's got some coffee made and there're oatmeal cookies in the jar."

"Could you bring it in here? We're trying to get this last strip up before lunch and clean up the mess. We'll start up the stairs this afternoon and hopefully get the hallway done before night. Tomorrow I think we'll begin painting if this rain lets up. If it doesn't then it'll keep most folks in at mealtimes so we'll do the dining room," Alice said.

"Sure thing," Sadie said.

In a few minutes she brought a tray bearing mugs of coffee and a plate of cookies. She set them on the register desk and leaned back watching for a few minutes. "I just love daisies. They make the room so cozy and bright. Did you pick them out, Ira?"

Alice rolled her eyes.

Ira blushed.

"No, Alice was already tangled up in paper when I arrived yesterday," he said. Lord, had it only been twenty four hours. It seemed like eternity. So much had happened so fast, he almost felt like he was back in the war where things changed by the minute and he never knew where he was going to be or what he was going to be doing from one second to the next.

"Oh, well, I do like it and you are doing such a wonderful job. I don't see a wrinkle anywhere. Lizzy, that would be my sister who lives next door with her passel of kids and a husband who thinks she's the most wonderful thing since creation, can't hang paper worth a dang. She's bought new paper for the living room but says if she hangs it there'll be more wrinkles in it than a shirt before it's ironed on Tuesday morning. Maybe we'll talk you into coming over and helping us out," she said.

"I doubt it. I've hired Ira and there's enough work here to keep him busy until Christmas when he's going to Mississippi to see his grandparents," Alice said coolly.

Sadie's blue eyes lit up like a bright summer sky. "Christmas?"

Alice read her mind in an instant. Sadie figured she had four months to work her wiles on Ira and perhaps he'd take her with him when he left Huttig. Another woman finds a husband; another good man bites the dust.

"Yes, that's right, and until then the Black Swan has every hour of his time," Alice said.

"But after he gets off work in the evenings I suppose his time is his own and he can hang paper for me if he wants," Sadie argued.

Alice shot her a drop-dead look, but it was wasted. The woman was busy making eyes at Ira. She could have made up a preposterous story saying that Ira had killed a dozen women with blue eyes, stabbed them to death with a kitchen butcher knife, and Sadie would have still batted her eyes at him.

Holy Mother of God, what was it about a tall lanky man with a job that had every single woman in Huttig out chasing him? Maybe Alice was in the wrong business. She should hire a man and charge all the women for a chance to get at him. After he was properly hitched, she could hire another and all the remaining women could come chasing that one. Maybe she could even get them to cook and clean for free for a chance to be Black Swan Man of the Month. It would be a fine marriage-making business.

"I'm afraid I'll be too busy to be working a second job," Ira finally said.

"Well, maybe you won't be too busy or tired for a little evening walk around town and an ice-cream cone sometime," Sadie said and then flaunted back into the kitchen.

"What in the hell has happened to this place?" Ira mumbled.

"What are you talking about?"

"When I left I was lucky someone even gave me a second look. Now there's women actin' mighty brazen, if you ask me," he said.

"It was the war. Shortage of men. Women working. Then men coming home and the women are ready for husbands. They've waited for the men to finish their war games and feel like they've taken backseat long enough. Things change. You're probably going to see a lot more before it's your time to die, Ira."

"I might but I don't have to like it."

CHAPTER FIVE

Alice would have rather been out on her bicycle scouting out new pictures to sketch, but Bridget had finally admitted she couldn't stand on her feet all day in the kitchen anymore. So that Friday morning found Sadie and Alice in the kitchen making peach cobbler and apple pies. Soup simmered in two huge pots on the stove. Corn bread was ready with tea towels thrown over it to keep the warmth in and the flies out. Tables were set and business was going on as usual.

At least until the kitchen door flew open and there stood Catherine as if she had appeared from thin air. Alice caught the measuring cup before it hit the ground and stared at her older sister as if she were an apparition.

"What are *you* doing here?" she asked bluntly.

Catherine hung her fancy hat on an apron

hook and took stock of the kitchen. "How exciting to see you too, Alice. The look on your face isn't surprise, it's something else. What's been going on that you don't want me to know? Quincy has a hard two weeks ahead of him getting his office set up and our new home won't be vacated for two more weeks so I've come home to help until Bridget has the baby. Looks like you've got things going fairly well. I'm going to see Bridget. Maybe she'll be more excited that I'm home."

"Catherine, I think I ought to tell you . . ." Alice began. She should have written like Ira said but somehow the words wouldn't go on the paper when she sent her weekly report to her older sister.

Catherine had her hand on the doorknob. She'd envisioned Alice being so excited about her surprise visit that she'd drop everything and rush to her with a big hug. Maybe it was Sadie in the kitchen that had stopped her, or maybe Alice was having one of her "I want to be outside" days or worse yet, one of her Jesus days. Those happened when she was in such a mood that Ella said even Jesus couldn't live with her.

The knob moved in her hand as someone pushed from the other side. Expecting Bridget she pulled the door open, only to find Ira McNewel not five inches away. Stunned, her eyes widened and her breath shortened.

"Catherine?" he said.

"You are dead," she whispered.

"And you are married. Congratulations." She took a step back. "What happened?"

He looked over her shoulder at Alice.

She threw up her hands in bewilderment. "I was going to tell her in the next letter. Now you can tell her in person."

"What is going on in here?" Bridget asked from the dining room doorway.

"Hello?" Catherine said, wondering even when she said it if there were more surprises on the way. What had happened to her predictable little home in the past four months?

Bridget crossed the room quickly and hugged her sister. "Catherine! How wonderful! How long can you stay? I want a hug. I'm big as a barn so your arms might not reach around me."

"How much longer?" Catherine asked, avoiding the issue of Ira.

"Doc says any day. I'm thinking maybe two weeks. Please say you can stay until she's born."

She turned around to stare at the man she'd been engaged to and who'd gone off to war only to die in a battle. "Of course I can stay. I came prepared for two weeks anyway. Now what is going on, Ira? You gave me quite a shock there. I thought I was seeing a ghost."

"Ira isn't dead. He's alive and he's working here for us until Christmas. Then he's going to Mississippi to see his grandparents. That's about it. Come on. I've got to show you the baby things." Bridget tugged her hand and led her out of the kitchen toward their quarters.

Catherine refused to budge. "Ira?"

"Bridget about summed it up. There was a mix-up. They thought I was dead but I was just badly injured."

She continued to stare. "I still can't believe you are standing in front of me."

"Just for another minute or two. I've got work to do," he said flatly. Catherine was still beautiful, more so than before, but he felt absolutely nothing when he looked at her. No big impulse to grab her in a fierce embrace; not a single thing other than admiring a lovely lady.

Bridget interrupted the brief scenario. "Come on. If you stand there gawking much longer the dinner crowd will be here."

Catherine allowed herself to be pulled into the lobby and from there through the door into their own living quarters. When Bridget let go of her hand she plopped down in a chair and exhaled loudly. She felt guilty for the relief in her heart. Had she known Ira wasn't dead, she would have never allowed herself to fall in love with Quincy. But she had and they were married and Ira was alive. Oh, what a mess, indeed.

Sadie looked over at Alice. "I'll finish up in here. You should have about thirty minutes before the first dinner crowd arrives. Go on, girl. Visit with your sister. You wantin' a cup of coffee and a cookie, Ira?"

Alice wanted to go but her feet were firmly planted. Did she leave Ira to fend for himself or make an excuse to stay?

"No, I just come in to ask Alice if she wants me to mend that piece of gingerbread up near the back eave of the house. It got wet and has some rot," he said.

"Yes, please. Do whatever you need to, Ira," Alice said.

"Then I'll get at it and let you ladies alone."

Alice made her way to the living room and melted into a chair beside Catherine with a long sigh. "I'm sorry. I meant to tell you about Ira and I didn't know you were coming back this soon. I thought I had a little

73

more time."

"I thought I was seeing ghosts." Catherine's voice was still shaky.

"So did I when I turned around on that ladder and fell right on top of him," Alice said, and then told her everything that had happened, both past and present. Ira's war story and what all had gone on in Huttig since she'd married Quincy and left at the beginning of summer.

Bridget placed a hand on her stomach. "Is it going to be awkward?"

"Yes, but we'll survive. He's living here?" Catherine asked.

Alice nodded.

"Well, I expect we'll all get through it once the shock wears off. Ira has always been a hard worker," she said.

"Oh, my yes," Bridget said. "He helped Alice hang the new wallpaper. Did you notice it? And he's about got the outside of the house painted. And two women are flirting with him."

Alice watched Catherine carefully for signs of jealousy. There were none, not a single flinch. "So is this going to be a problem with Quincy. I can pay Ira and send him on to his grandparents' tomorrow."

"I'll tell Quincy for sure when he calls me

tonight but I don't think it'll be a problem. Ira was dead and I buried him in my heart. I'm in love with Quincy and he trusts me, I'm sure."

"There'll be talk," Bridget said.

Alice actually blushed. "So what?"

"Why are you turning red? Have there been problems?" Catherine asked.

Bridget told her the story of the day Mabel and Dottie caught Alice lying on top of Ira when the bicycle upset both of them.

Alice threw up her hands. "You're taking this almighty well. I figured you'd swoon or throw dishes or something other than just accepting it. Great God, Catherine, you were engaged to him and he's not dead. It's kind of like that story Elizabeth put out, remember?"

"It was a shock. I've got to admit that much, but looking back with what I know now, Ira was more like a brother than a husband. There was no passion; there were no sparks, Alice. Not like I have with Quincy."

"Sparks?" Alice asked.

"Yes, sparks. Ira and I would have been a very comfortable couple. We would have raised kids and stayed together but it wouldn't have been a passionate love like I have with Quincy," Catherine declared.

"You mean it's like we talked about that day before you left?" Bridget asked. "There's really a possibility that there's a man out there that makes your heart race just kissing him?"

Catherine smiled. She was the oldest of the three O'Shea daughters. Her hair was a rich, deep burgundy, the color of a sugar maple leaf in the fall, her eyes a rich olive green, and there wasn't a freckle on her face. She carried her self tall and proud and had always been the responsible one of the girls, even when they were young. But she hadn't been the first one to have a husband, Bridget had. And yet, she was finding out quickly that some married folks did not have the kind of passionate love she and Quincy shared. A marriage license or vows said before a preacher didn't come with passion guaranteed to bloom from the night of the honeymoon until the moment of death. Either it was there or it wasn't; and it wasn't with Ira.

"When did you feel these sparks?" Alice asked. The middle child who'd been tagged fey back when she was a child, she had been a carrottop as a teenager but her hair had grown darker in the past few years. It would never be as dark as Catherine's or as light as Bridget's strawberry blond hair. Her eyes were also that strange in-between shade of green. Not as dark as Catherine's, nor as light as Bridget's big round aqua eyes.

"From day one and I fought it all the way up to the point when I told him he was going to kiss me and then propose," Catherine said.

Bridget clamped a hand over her mouth. "You didn't!"

"I did. He was going to Galveston and I was too damn jealous to let him take a make-believe wife," Catherine told them.

Alice filed away the conversation to a later date when she could replay every single word. One thing for dang sure, Ira didn't feel like a brother to her. But then, even if she did feel sparks and electricity, it didn't mean he did. He'd made the comment that she might have been his sister if he'd married Catherine, so that's probably how he felt.

"Well, I expect I'd best get on back to the kitchen," she said.

"And I'll change into a work dress and go with you. I'm glad I got here today. Bridget, you are too big to be in the kitchen," Catherine said.

"I know it and that's why we trained Sadie, but we're glad for the help and really glad you're home for a while. It's been lonely without you. The bedroom is lonely at night without you in your bed and all three of us discussing the day as we fall asleep," Bridget said.

Catherine grinned. "I miss that part of the day sometimes too. Tell the truth, I thought you'd miss me in other ways. Quincy said you two could run it if I wasn't here and be danged if he hasn't proven to be right, but don't tell him. I hate like the devil when he wins."

Ira pulled the nails holding the gingerbread up on the back side of the house and carefully carried the piece down the ladder to a worktable he'd made from two sawhorses and an old board he'd found in the shed. He was measuring when the back door opened and Alice stepped out. Now there was a woman who could make his heart skip a beat and there wasn't a thing he could do about it.

"What do you want?" he asked.

"Hey, don't be mad at me because your long-lost love popped in for two weeks and you have to be in her presence all that time. It's not my fault," she snapped.

"I told you before the way I feel about her," he smarted right back.

"Words and actions are two different

78

things, Ira McNewel."

"What does that mean?"

"Just think about it but don't set your brain on fire and smoke damage your ears," she said.

"Why are you being mean to me? I didn't do anything."

"I'm not being mean. You are. I just came out here to tell you the dinner crowd is gone and you'd best come on in and make yourself a plate before we put it all away for supper. Catherine has gone back to our room so it won't be awkward. You never did miss a meal before so what am I to think?"

"That I was busy," he said defensively.

"Oh, sure," she quipped.

"Why are you fighting with me?"

"I think fighting is a two-way street. We're both fighting," she told him.

"But why?"

"If you don't know I'm danged sure not going to tell you." She slammed the back door behind her.

He ate alone at a dining room table near the kitchen door and listened to Sadie sing while she washed dishes. She was an attractive and hardworking woman so why couldn't his heart do double-time when he was around her? Oh, no, it had to save that for the very worst woman he could ever be attracted to.

He made plans as he shoveled soup into his mouth. It would take at least three more days to finish the painting job. Catherine was home and could help with what needed to be done and if they wanted man-type work done, they could hire another handyman. Because when the painting job was finished, Ira McNewel was boarding the train to Mississippi and never looking back.

Chapter Six

Alice braced her back against her mother's tombstone and attempted to sketch a squirrel poking his head out of a hole in a tall pine tree. She couldn't get it right so she shut her eyes and flipped the page to a blank one. A blush bloomed on her cheeks when she began to draw Ira again. Lately, he was the only subject she could keep focused on and it made her both angry and sad.

It had been so easy to fall back into the old pattern and rut when Catherine came home. Catherine had always been the strong one of the three so when she stepped into the Black Swan everything went right back to depending on her strength. But for the first time in her life, Alice didn't want to wallow in that familiar old rut. She wanted Ira to see her as just as smart, well-adjusted, and tough a woman as Catherine. Those were the qualities that had drawn him to Catherine and he'd be looking for someone equally as bright when he started looking for a woman, not the village idiot.

She held the drawing out away from her. The eyes weren't quite right. They had light and life but they were looking beyond Alice, not at her. She liked it when he looked right at her; liked the gentleness in his eyes at those times. The mouth was right. She shut her eyes and imagined what it would be like to have those lips touch hers. Even if so brief a moment and just barely qualifying as a kiss. Warmth spread through her body and heat filled her face. She snapped her eyes open and looked around to see if anyone had seen her actually pucker her lips together waiting for the kiss that would never arrive.

"Now I really feel like a fool," she mumbled. A clap of thunder jerked her back to reality. She hurriedly put her drawing tools into the case and squinted up at the sky. She needed eyeglasses for sure. Up close, when she was drawing or reading, everything was in focus and fine. But looking across the room at Ira or trying to focus on the daisies on the new wallpaper from a distance was a different story. Maybe she'd always needed glasses and that's what had started the crazy notion that she was dim-witted in the first place. That blank look that really meant she couldn't see what she was looking at didn't mean she was stupid, but rather nearsighted. Why, oh why hadn't she mentioned it way back then?

"Because you didn't want the other little girls to call you four eyes," she muttered as she picked her bicycle up from the ground and settled into the seat.

It had been difficult enough being in the middle of the two pretty O'Shea girls; Catherine on one end with her dark red hair and flawless complexion, Bridget on the other with her petite beauty that made men want to protect her. To have worn glasses too would have really set Alice aside as the ugly duckling in the house of lovely black swans. But the time had come to accept the fact she couldn't see and to do something about it. She'd taken the test in the Sears Catalog and had the order ready for number ten glasses. It had laid on her dresser for six weeks and she'd been about to send it when Ira showed up, risen from the dead.

She was thinking about how badly she was going to hate wearing eyeglasses and how much she'd look like a plain-Jane old maid when lightning streaked through the sky and hit a tree not ten feet in front of her. The limb that snapped from high up on the tree fell like it was in a hurry to get to the ground, the branches hitting Alice and knocking her off her bike. The earth came up to meet her ever so slowly and the last thing she saw before the next clap of thunder was a tombstone, the letters becoming clearer and clearer as her head got closer and closer to the gray granite.

She had no idea how much time had elapsed when she opened her eyes. It might have been seconds, minutes, or even hours. There was a hard rain falling and sitting up was impossible. Something was pinning her feet solidly to the ground. She glanced down but all she could see were tree branches and pine needles. Her eyelids eased shut and the comfort of blackness took her away from the pain in her head and leg.

When she came to the second time she was wet to the skin and more alert, taking stock of what was going on around her. She sat up in a hazy swirl of bright colors and tried to push the tree limb away from her leg, but it was too heavy. She lay back slowly, careful to keep her head away from the tombstone. Reaching up to gingerly touch the throb above her right eye, she was amazed to find a scrape the size of a silver dollar but no blood. It didn't feel like it needed to be sewn but more like a mushy spot where she'd bumped the slick granite.

A dam of tears broke loose and flowed freely down her pale cheeks. "I'm so sorry, Mommy. I should have told you I couldn't see," she sobbed like a little girl.

Suddenly the rain stopped and the clouds above her parted. Rays descended like a stairway from heaven to earth, slanted ever so slightly. She cocked her head and squinted. Was heaven beckoning her to join her mother and father? Surely she hadn't hit her head that hard. There was no blood. And her ankle hurt but she couldn't see bones sticking out of her skin. The pine trees glistened in the bright sunlight. The tombstones around her were washed clean. Still in all that beauty, she was simply not strong enough to move that blasted tree from her legs.

Catherine could have moved the limb. Lord, she would have just given it one of her frowns and the sorry thing would have sprouted wings and flown off her leg. Alice conjured up her most evil glare but the limb didn't move an inch. She could die right there in the cemetery. That thought struck her as hilarious and she began to giggle.

Death was no stranger to Union County, Arkansas. The flu had certainly shown them that they had no control over the number of days a person had on the earth. In a matter of hours they could be snatched away to eternity. What better place to go than the cemetery? Besides, there was that little matter of Bridget's husband, Ralph, and where he ended up. The whole thing could be poetic justice.

A pine tree, the thing that brought the O'Shea family to southern Arkansas, falling on her in the cemetery: irony or oxymoron? Either way, she was pinned beneath one and there wasn't a dang thing she could do about it. Trees — the evidence of life's continuous circle. Big ones were harvested for the lumber mill; new ones were planted; diseased ones were destroyed. It was just another instance of life's cycle. Babies took the place of the elderly who were buried. From womb to tomb life went on in joy or sorrow. Her mind ran around in circles thinking of death, birth, babies, old people, and back again to the tombstones surrounding her.

"I'm not old," she whimpered as she lay back on the wet earth again.

But you are diseased so you must be destroyed, her conscience argued. *You can't see and you aren't as bright as Catherine or Bridget. Your time has come, Alice. Bid goodbye to this world and climb the sunrays to heaven. That is, if a person gets to go to heaven after what you did with Ralph.*

She forced her eyes open. "I will not. I'm not giving up that danged easy."

Thunder woke Catherine. Storms often brought babies according to the old wives' tales so she immediately looked across the room. Bridget was sleeping soundly, her big belly looking like a huge balloon under the sheets. Alice's bed was empty but that wasn't unusual. Alice was an early riser, often up and about at daybreak with her sketching. She'd said she loved art so much she'd make time for it even if she had to give up sleep. Evidently she had that morning.

Catherine stretched and pulled on a robe before wandering out into the lobby. She opened the front door and leaned against the jamb, watching it rain. Lightning lit up the early morning sky and thunder followed. It was pretty as long as she was on the inside looking out. She hoped that Alice was holed up at the Commercial Hotel in the dining room having a cup of coffee with the patrons who arose at the crack of dawn. Surely she wasn't out in the storm; even Alice had the good sense to find shelter at the first strike of lightning.

"Another rainy day," Ira said so close behind her she could actually feel his breath on the sensitive skin of her neck.

She jumped. "Looks like it."

It had been a week since she'd come home and she missed Quincy horribly. He phoned for just a minute every other night and she'd received two letters. Neither helped her sleep at night nor took away the emptiness.

Ira stepped back and busied himself with papers on the countertop. "Didn't mean to startle you."

"It's all right. We need to talk and this is as good a time as any. Come and sit and let's get it over with," Catherine said.

Ira followed her to a seating group and took a chair close to the settee where she sat. "You never did mince words."

"It's not my style and you know it," she said. "Ira, you are better off without me. I didn't love you like a woman should love a husband."

He smiled.

Mercy, he wasn't supposed to grin. She'd just broken his heart.

"I know, Catherine. We would have made a good couple but not a passionate one. I could have lived with that before I almost died. Neither of us would have known anything but Huttig and sawmills, hotel work, and we would have gone on to be old people together, but there was no passion."

"How did you get so smart? Was there another woman over there?"

"I thought there was but I was wrong. It was just passion rearing its head and telling me that I wanted more than a woman who was just my friend. I wanted one who made me see stars when I kissed her and made my heart race when I touched her fingertips."

"And he's also a poet," she said.

"Naw, I never was one for words."

"Thank you, Ira, for understanding and for being honest."

"Same back to you. Where's Alice? Bridget all right this morning?"

"Alice is off sketching somewhere, I guess. Bridget is fine. The storm didn't shake the baby loose. I'm terrified it will be a boy and she'll refuse to even look at it. There's not one thing back there for a boy. She's even embroidered rosebuds on the diapers."

He didn't hear a word about the baby. His eyes were fixed on the raging rain and visualizing Alice out there in the electrical storm. "I'm going to go find her."

"Who?" Catherine asked.

"Alice."

"Why? She's got enough sense to get out

of the rain, Ira. She's not stupid, you know."

"Not as much as she's let everyone believe all these years. But something isn't right. I can feel it in my bones," he said.

The front door literally blew open and a tall, muscular man appeared as if the wind had deposited him in the lobby without any effort at all. Raindrops clung to his thick brown hair and he wiped the wet from his freshly shaven cheeks just before he removed an overcoat. Under it he wore khaki-colored trousers and a blue work shirt that had not been ironed. Old creases were faded on the sleeves but the rest of the shirt attested to the fact that the man hadn't used an iron.

"Catherine?" He cocked his head to one side and flashed a wide grin.

"Baxter?" She was amazed that she remembered his name.

He hung his wet coat on a hat rack behind the door and quickly crossed the room to sit down beside her on the settee. "I told you I'd come back and we'd go out to dinner or for a walk. So here I am."

Ira chuckled. "Good luck."

Catherine shook a finger at him. "You stay out of this."

"Baxter, I got married at the first of the summer. I'm just here to help out until my sister has the baby."

"Well, dang, if it wasn't for bad luck, I'd have no luck at all. Please don't tell me the Black Swan is booked solid. I do need a room for the night. My train leaves tomorrow for Memphis."

"We do have a room and breakfast will be served in about an hour if you are interested," she said.

"I'll take it and trust me, I'm interested. Where's your other sister? The one who was always running round with a sketch pad?"

"Out hunting something to draw, I suppose," Catherine said.

Ira quickly made his way to the door, donned a rain slicker that Alice kept hanging there, and slipped out the front door.

"You could have written me a postcard or something," Baxter pouted.

"Never crossed my mind once I fell in love with Quincy."

"The detective? You fell in love with the detective? That's impossible."

"Oh, it's possible."

Sadie pushed her way through the door, hanging up her slicker and removing rain boots. "It's a good day out there if you're a duck. I'm thinking we'd best check on the price of some gopher wood and commence to building an ark. Oh, hello!" She stopped dead in her tracks in the middle of the floor and literally ogled Baxter.

"Hello to you. And you are?"

"I'm Sadie. I've been helping these ladies out with the hotel while Miss Bridget is laid up. And you are?"

"Baxter Wright. Came through here last spring and promised Miss Catherine I'd be back around to do some courting, only the detective done beat my time. I'll be spending the day and night. Don't suppose you'd care to take a walk after supper?"

So much for wounded male pride, Catherine thought. It was the fastest-healing emotion in the world. The only thing that it took for a full recovery was an available woman to appear in time for a healthy dose of flirting and preening. She'd never noticed how much Baxter looked like a peacock or acted like one. She rolled her eyes toward the ceiling as she made her way back to the bedroom to get dressed.

The rain had slowed down by the time Ira reached the Commercial Hotel close to downtown Huttig. He stepped inside the door, wiped his feet on the rug, and felt a dozen eyes on him. Men reading the morning paper after breakfast were scattered in the lobby; women corralled children who had too much energy to be inside.

The desk clerk raised his voice above a crying baby. "Help you with something, Ira?"

"Seen Alice?"

"Not this morning."

"Thanks." Ira nodded and went back outside.

The clouds parted, letting sun rays filter down between the holes. Ira pinched the bridge of his nose and tried to put himself in Alice's shoes. Where would she go? What had she been working on lately?

"That danged squirrel at the cemetery," he mumbled.

He went directly to Ella O'Shea's gravesite but Alice wasn't there. The whole cemetery was a muddy mess with the effects of the hard rain, and he didn't see any footprints leading to or from the grave. He shaded his eyes against the glaring sunlight trying to dry up every drop of moisture the clouds had forced upon the earth. That's when he saw the downed tree limb.

"No, surely she wouldn't be . . . ," he muttered as he headed that way.

A faint giggle put him into a dead run.

He dropped to his knees beside her. "Alice?"

"Is that you, Ira? I'm not afraid of storms. I'm the air. Did you know that? I'm the air.

93

Catherine is the dirt but I'm the air and I'm not afraid of storms. But that dang tree fell on me. I can't get out of here. Isn't that the funniest thing you've ever heard?"

He was everywhere at once. Checking her head to make sure she wasn't bleeding since she was talking out of her mind. Using his bare hands he dug a hole beneath her pinned leg and carefully pulled her free. He propped her up in his lap and made her raise her arms, wiggle her fingers, raise her left leg, and shake her foot. That's as far as it went. When she lifted her right leg, she winced and began to cry.

"It hurts. I'm not afraid of air because I am air. Did I already tell you that, Ira? Are you for real or am I dreaming again? You could be a mirage. Don't tell Catherine. She thinks you are dead. Can you help me home? Momma will fix my leg. Momma can fix anything. She takes care of Ralph, you know. We couldn't just trust anyone with him but Momma won't tell. Shhhh!" She placed her fingers over her lips to let him know she'd just told him a choice secret.

He removed her right boot to find a black-and-blue ankle but no bones protruding through the skin. He let out a whoosh of air that he wasn't even aware he was holding.

"Are you going to cut it off? Don't make

a mess. Momma doesn't like messes. Ralph wasn't so very messy. He shouldn't have hit Bridget, you know. I didn't like him and I hope the devil torments him. I hope he has to clean the outhouses in hell. That's what I hope Ralph has to do for all eternity. Did I tell you that I don't like Ralph?"

"Yes, you did. You aren't going to be able to walk on that leg and I'm afraid to leave you here so I'm going to pick you up ever very gently and carry you back to the hotel. Will you be still and not wiggle?"

"I'm the air. I'll be light as air. Just don't cut my foot off when we get there. Tell Momma to fix it and did I tell you Catherine got married? Well, she did. I knew you weren't dead. If you'd been dead I would have known. The air knows things the dirt doesn't. But I didn't tell her because she wanted to marry Quincy and besides, she never listens to me anyway. She thinks dirt is more powerful than air but it's not. Air can make thunder and lightning and she's afraid of storms. I'm not afraid of storms because I am just like a storm. Did I tell you I can't see?"

He gathered her up into his arms and began to walk as fast as possible toward town. "Oh, my lord. Are you blind?"

"No, I'm not blind. I can see the trees.

95

They are green and they have water drops on them and that dang squirrel is sitting on a limb. I can hear him barking but he's a bit of a blur. Look at the ornery critter. If I had Momma's little gun, I'd blow him out of that tree and make squirrel dumplings out of him once I have some eyeglasses and learn to shoot. Teach him to tear around and not be still for me to sketch him, it would. And there's a buzzard. Do you think that old ugly bird was coming to the cemetery to eat my eyes out?"

Ira shuddered.

"Too bad, you vulture. Ira is taking me home to Momma," she shouted to the bird.

"Then you can see. Why did you say you couldn't see?"

"Because I can't. I need eyeglasses but I didn't want to tell anyone because I'm already the ugly duckling. I'm going to buy them someday and then I'll see better but not today. Today I'm going to watch them cut my foot off and fix it. Can they sew it back on when they get it fixed, Ira?"

"They are not going to cut your foot off," he said gruffly.

She began to weep. "But I don't want to be blind and crippled both. Stop laughing at me, Ralph. You know I hate you. Go back to cleaning the outhouse and leave me alone."

"I'm not Ralph."

"No, silly man. You are Ira and you aren't dead. I'm going to sleep awhile now. I can hear your heart beating. I could always hear it. That's why I knew you weren't dead. I could hear your heart." She drifted off into a fitful sleep where she murmured, giggling and sobbing intermittently.

"Catherine!" he yelled from the lobby and wasn't a bit surprised to see her blanch when she came from the dining room.

Her feet had lead in them and she moved as if they were stuck in mire. "My God, what has happened?"

"A tree fell on her and she couldn't get out. I don't think she's bleeding. Most of it is mud but she's talking crazy and her foot is either broken or badly sprained. Send someone after the doctor. I'll —"

"Lay her on the settee right there, Ira, and then would you please go for the doctor while I clean her up?" Catherine took over in a few words. It was her place. It was what she did. After all, she was as steadfast as the Irish land from which her parents had come from.

Alice looked beyond Ira and Catherine at Baxter who stood at the bottom of the stairs. "No! Ira's not going anywhere. Who are you? Are you the doctor who is going to sew my foot back on? I am a very, very rich woman and I will pay you well to sew my foot on right. Don't make a mistake and make sure all my toes work. Someday I'm going to dance at my wedding and show old Ralph that I'm not ugly. He cleans outhouses in hell, you know. Momma is taking care of that. Where is Momma, Catherine?"

She held on to Ira's hand with a grip that defied life. "You must stay and make sure the doctor does his job right. Catherine, I'm not afraid of storms because I am air. It wasn't the storm. It was that danged stupid squirrel."

"Concussion?" Sadie asked.

"Looks like it," Ira said. "Seen a few in the war."

"Baxter, would you go for the doctor, please? His office is right next door to the Commercial Hotel," Catherine asked.

"Be right glad to help," Baxter said. His mind was jumping from one dollar sign to the next. If Alice was telling the truth about being very, very rich then the woman he'd left behind in Louisiana could wait forever. She was just plain rich, not very, very. Baxter Wright was looking for the easy life and it didn't matter if the woman was slightly

98

touched. That could actually be a blessing because she wouldn't know where he spent his nights and she'd be so much easier to control.

Oh, yes, Baxter had surely done the right thing when he stopped by the Black Swan for a night. This was even better than if Catherine had still been available.

Chapter Seven

Somewhere in the back of Alice's mind she knew Catherine was washing mud from her hair and face. Somewhere off in a land where reality was a myth she heard the doctor tell Catherine that her foot was not broken but badly sprained and she would be using crutches for a few weeks.

It was as if she heard the words and felt the warmth of the water flowing through her hair and into the bucket on the floor, but those things didn't matter. What did matter was digging the loose dirt so they could put Ralph's body in the hole. Bridget shouldn't have to use a shovel but she'd insisted. So did Catherine. So the three of them sunk the shovel into the dirt and piled it out to the side. When they finished Alice insisted they go back to the hotel just in case someone came by. Everything they did would be in vain if they were to get caught and Bridget would go to jail. After all, who would believe she was innocent? Ralph was a Contiello and they had power in big places.

"People are used to seeing me out and about after dark. It won't create a stir if I'm walking home in the moonlight," she had said.

She slept all day and night but when morning dawned the next day she began to thrash about, mumbling about Ralph being a worthless human and Ira not being dead. She would declare in a clear voice that she was pushing the tree off her foot and the next minute she'd be whining in a three-year-old's voice begging for chocolate cake for breakfast.

"Is she in pain?" Bridget asked.

"Doc says that she's got a concussion. She may be five years old and fighting with some child at school or trying to learn to ride her bicycle. He says that the brain is a delicate thing. I just hope it's only a concussion and that her brain isn't affected so much that she'll die from that," Catherine said.

"Go home. I'll put the dirt all back. I can do this. Take Bridget home," Alice said clearly.

"Oh my God, she's reliving that night," Bridget paled.

"We'll have to keep her isolated until she

comes to her senses," Catherine said.

"Sorry stinking excuse for a man. I'll tell them I killed you before I let Bridget take the blame," Alice said very plainly.

Bridget's eyes filled with tears. "I wouldn't let her. You know that, don't you?"

Catherine pinned up her hair as she talked. "Of course I know it. She's talking out of her head because of that bump she got. No one is going to take blame for an accident. Stop crying and pick up your embroidery. You can watch her and I'll get on back in the kitchen with Sadie. By now news is out about the accident and you can bet everyone in the whole dang town will be coming in for lunch and supper just to pick up the gossip. I'm glad today is home-made soup day. There's always plenty of that if we have a big crowd. Maybe I'll get Ira to step in and help us if we get swamped."

Alice's eyes popped wide open and she stared at the ceiling. How on earth had she gone from filling in a grave for Ralph to lying flat on her back in her bedroom? "I was dreaming, I think. A tree fell on me and I had this terrible dream about that night."

"Yes, you did," Bridget said.

Alice's gaze never faltered. "I want Ira. Bring him in here."

"I will not!" Bridget said.

"Then I'm going out there. I need to talk to him," Alice sat up. The walls billowed like curtains being blown inside from a strong wind. She flopped back down on her back. "Call the pretty doctor back. I think I broke my head."

"The doctor is seventy years old, bald-headed, and chubby," Bridget said.

"No, the pretty one. The one who was here when Ira brought me home," she said.

"That's Baxter Wright. He's not a doctor," Bridget argued.

"Then go get him."

"I'm not having a man in our bedroom. Lord, Momma would roll over in her grave," Bridget said.

Alice began to giggle. "I can just see Momma trying to roll over in her grave."

"It is pretty funny," Catherine said. "Now, I'm going in to help Sadie. You two can visit and Alice, your head isn't broken. Neither is your foot. It's just got a bad sprain. When you can sit up without getting dizzy, you can sit on the porch. I'm sure everyone in town is going to want to talk to you about the accident."

"Save me from a fate worse than death," Alice declared.

Bridget narrowed her eyes. "What?"

"A tree fell on me in the cemetery. I sure

don't want to tell the story a dozen times. Put me on a train and send me to that beach where you and Quincy went. It's not fair that I have to stay in the house or else put up with nosy neighbors. Oh, no! Mabel will tell me it's the devil punishing me for riding on the handlebars with Ira," she moaned as the full effect of what might happen sank in.

"You were talking crazy just minutes ago," Bridget said. "Are you all right now?"

Alice raised a hand and carefully felt her head. "It still aches but I can remember what happened."

Catherine slipped out the door with a wave. They'd been raised in the Black Swan hotel and everything had been routine and business until six months ago when their mother died, one of the last fatalities of the flu epidemic. Now with every day there was a new catastrophe. First it was the ordeal with Ralph and the absolute terror that caused. Then just when they thought they had put his disappearance behind them Quincy arrived with his detective nose and the snooping began. They'd finally gotten him convinced that their story about Bridget's abusive husband was the solid truth, which it was — they'd just left out one important detail. That of him falling to his death and the three of them hiding his body. Then Catherine comes home for a quiet two weeks to help with the new baby and finds Ira, resurrected from the dead. And Baxter: What was he up to?

Ira was crossing the lobby from the dining room when he caught sight of her. "How's Alice?"

"She's alert and fussing to get out of bed. I think the worst is over," Catherine answered.

"Want me to go carry her out to the porch? She'll get crazy if she has to stay inside all day."

"I'll be glad to sit with her," Baxter said from one of the settees.

"I thought you were leaving this morning," Catherine said.

"Change of plans. I'm not in a hurry and my ticket can be used anytime. Just charge me up for a week on the register. I'll pay in advance if you need me to or else I'll settle up when I leave."

"You can pay however you want. But both of you listen to me very closely. No one goes into our bedroom. Bridget wouldn't like that," Catherine said emphatically.

"Oh, you share? I just figured there were three bedrooms in that part," Baxter said.

"No, we share. She'll probably find her

way out sometime today with her crutches. I'm going to help Sadie with breakfast. What's on your agenda today, Ira?"

"I'm finished with the painting so I suppose I'll be working in the basement," he said.

"I have nothing to do. When Alice is ready to come out of her room, I'll keep her company on the porch," Baxter said.

Alice was ravenous at lunch. She ate two bowls of soup, three slabs of corn bread, and two pieces of pie, after which she dressed herself with no help, picked up the old crutches her father had used when he fell off the shed roof twenty years before, and thumped her way out to the porch.

"Might as well get it over with. Can't run from it but I can sure tell them all where to go and how to get there," she said.

Bridget hauled her rotund body out of the chair and followed Alice to the porch. "I think I'd better go with you."

The sun had come out with vengeance, determined to dry up all the effects of the rain. Oppressive humidity hung in the air. The latecomers for lunch were just leaving and the ladies gasped when the warm, moist air hit them in the face as they left the cool confines of the hotel lobby. Most of them didn't tarry long on the porch. A few simple words and they were off to their own homes where they could change their good dresses into soft, worn cotton day dresses.

"Thank you, Lord, for giving everyone just a little taste of what hell could be like so they'll get on out of here," Alice whispered.

"Honey, God gave us the rain. The devil brought the heat," Bridget grinned.

"Then bless his little fork-tailed heart," Alice said.

Baxter melted his muscular frame into a rocking chair beside Alice. "Who are you blessing?"

"That would be the devil himself," Alice said.

He frowned. "Are you all right?"

"I'm fine. Where is Ira?"

"Working, I suppose. He came up all dirty and nasty from the basement and ate in the kitchen with Sadie. Said he wasn't fit to be sitting in the dining room with paying customers," Baxter answered.

Crimson flooded Alice's face. Sadie was flirting again, trying to get Ira to take her out on a date or at least for a walk through town so she could show everyone that he was interested.

Ira rounded the house and sat on the front

steps. "Did I hear my name?"

"You did. I've been trying to find you," Alice said.

"Well, here I am. How are you feeling?"

"I'm fine and I wish everyone would just shut up about me. I feel like a fool enough as it is with a tree pinning me to the ground for hours. People probably think I just stood there and let it fall on me."

"I can see that the accident really sweetened up your mood," Ira smarted off right back at her.

"What did you do with my sketch pad?"

"I didn't do a thing with your drawing paper. I just dug a hole under your leg, eased you out of the mess you were in, and carried you home. The last thing on my mind was your stupid paper. I thought you had a broke leg or your head was bashed in. Couldn't tell if it was mud or blood. I dang sure wasn't thinkin' about squirrels on your drawing pad."

Alice pointed at him, her finger shaking and her eyes drawn down into mere slits. "Don't you take that tone with me."

"Hey, you're the one who got up on a high horse. I just came around to check on you. I'll go on back to work now that I see you're back to your normal hateful self."

Baxter gloated.

"I've never been hateful to you," she said.

"You started out hateful. Threw yourself down off that ladder on me, knocked the breath right out of my lungs, then asked why I wasn't dead. Is that hateful or what, Bridget?" Ira asked.

"I'm not getting in the middle of your fight," Bridget said.

"Sounds like you take things the wrong way, old man," Baxter said.

Alice glared at him. "This isn't your fight either so shut up and go away."

Bridget slapped at the air beside her sister's arm. "Alice!"

"Don't you Alice me. I'm not stupid or dumb like everyone thinks I am. I can't see worth a dang but I've got a mind and I'm good at what I do, and Ira has lost my drawing pad and I'm mad at him. That doesn't mean Baxter can talk mean to him. I can but you can't." She turned her eyes from her sister to Baxter, who was grinning like some kind of idiotic fool.

"I'm going back to work," Ira said.

"No, you are going to the cemetery to find my drawing pad. I want it and that's what you are going to do," Alice said.

Ira folded his arms across his chest. "You hired me to work on this hotel, not run around the countryside hunting for wet paper."

"I am your boss and you'll do what I say."

"Yes, ma'am. It all pays the same, doesn't it? But if you continue in this vein, honey, I'll be out of here long before Christmas."

"Don't you threaten me, Ira McNewel."

"Don't you lord it over me, Alice O'Shea. I work for you but you are not going to act like you are some kind of queen and I'm nothing but a peasant."

"Go find my drawing pad," Alice said between clenched teeth. This wasn't at all the way she'd planned on asking him to help her. She'd figured she'd thank him for his efforts, ask nicely, and he'd be off to do her bidding without a word. She sure didn't mean for it to turn into a war in front of Baxter and Bridget.

"Yes, ma'am. If I can't find it are you going to have me beheaded?"

"Yes, I am, and I'll wield the sword myself," she raised her voice.

Ira saluted smartly and swiveled about on his toes like a soldier. He held his shoulders high and his chin up as he limped out of the yard and off to the cemetery to do the Irish queen's bidding. He'd find the drawing pad and if it wasn't covered with mud then he'd make dang sure it was before he brought it back to her. She had no right to be so downright mean and hateful to him, and in front of other people to boot. She hadn't even said a polite thank-you for all he'd done. Granted she wasn't much heavier than a sack of grain, but still he'd carried her all the way back to the hotel and paced the floor while the doctor examined her leg and her head. She had absolutely no right to treat him like a slave.

Alice set her mouth in a firm line and literally glared at the lilac bush beside the porch. If it had had a heart, it would have shrunk down into the wet earth and hidden from the force of her anger.

Catherine carried a cardboard fan with her to the nearest rocking chair. "What's all the yelling about?"

"Alice just put the hired help in his place," Baxter said.

"You did what?" Catherine asked.

"She and Ira are fighting. What does that tell you?" Bridget giggled.

"It doesn't tell her one thing except that I hired him to do what I said and he didn't want to go find my sketch pad where I left it in the cemetery," Alice said. "So I made him do what I said because I'm his boss." Lord, she was miserable. Winning a fight sure didn't bring about peace.

She jerked her head around to melt Baxter with the heat of her wrath. "For your information, Baxter Wright, he's not the hired help. He's a dear family friend and Catherine was engaged to him, but then he died and she married Quincy. He's been nice enough to help us around here until Christmas and then he's going to his grandparents' place in Mississippi, so don't you be calling him the hired help."

"Looks to me like that bump on the head brought out some hidden feelings, didn't it, Alice?" Catherine said.

"Oh, don't you go getting all preachy with me. You might be dirt and all solid and dependable but I'm air, and without air, none of you would survive after three minutes."

"What are you talking about?" Baxter asked.

"This isn't your fight. You'd best stay out of it," Bridget said.

"But I thought . . . ," he started.

"That's where all you miserable men get into trouble. You think! Don't you know that's beyond your capabilities? You weren't put on the earth to think. You were put here to kill the hogs and steers. Work and put food on the table. Women think. Men don't have that power. We let them think they do to keep peace and harmony on the earth, but don't for one minute think that you are able to outthink a woman," Alice said.

"Hey, now." Baxter attempted to defend his position as a man.

Alice put the palm of her hand toward his face. "Don't even try. You don't have enough words to argue with me today. Ira is my friend and an old friend of this family. You have no right to call him the hired help."

"You treated him like a slave and I can't call him hired help?" Baxter's face burned with indignation. Even all the money in the world wouldn't make it worth listening to that kind of talk every day. Whoever made the comment that a man who married for money certainly earned it was a genius.

"Now you're talkin' sense," Alice said.

Baxter threw up his hands and walked off the porch and down the street.

"You must like Ira a lot," Catherine said.

"The way she just treated him, I sure wouldn't want to be in his shoes if she didn't like him," Bridget said.

"I don't like Ira, not like that." Alice had the strongest urge to cross her fingers behind her back.

"Good. It would be very awkward to have him in the family since I was engaged to him," Catherine said.

"Well, by all means, let's not let the dirt in the family be one bit awkward. I can always be the dumb old maid of the O'Shea family but I must never marry because it would make my sister who is the pure salt of the earth feel awkward," Alice said.

Catherine headed for the door. "I'm going back in the house. You are picking fights."

"I'm right behind you." It took three jump-starts before Bridget cleared the chair but she followed, leaving Alice alone on the porch.

"Good. I don't need either one of you," she said.

"What's the matter with her?" Bridget whispered when they were back in the bedroom.

"She's fighting her feelings for Ira."

"No!"

"Oh, yes."

"But you said if she liked him it would be awkward," Bridget said.

"Yes, I did," Catherine singsonged.

"I'll never understand you. I was married and I never acted or felt like that," Bridget said.

"You were married, little sister. You never were in love," Catherine said.

"I'm not so sure I ever want to be if it makes me act like you did when you were fighting with Quincy, or like Alice is . . . Oh, now I see what you are talking about." Bridget's eyes widened out and she covered her mouth with her hand.

The steamy humidity was nothing compared to Ira's temper as he stomped down the road toward the cemetery. He mumbled about how he'd like to slap the meanness right out of Alice and knew the whole time he was grumbling that he'd never lay a hand on her pretty face.

Stood right up to you. Ain't nearly as witless as folks has made her out to be.

"Don't know why she's let people believe that of her. She's bright as the sun and pretty as a picture. And I danged sure don't know why I even care. She's too blasted stubborn for this old feller." He headed toward the fallen tree branch to begin his search for the sketch pad. It wasn't as if she couldn't afford a new one. He'd have even bought one himself if she would have just let him get on back to remodeling the basement.

He pushed aside pine needles but didn't see anything of an oversized writing tablet. Then he saw a few papers stuck to a tombstone. He pulled the pieces off to find smeared black streaks of what might have been a squirrel in a tree, or a cloud just before it formed into a tornado. Or it could have been nothing more than paper that had been used to wipe the rain from the tombstone.

However, his boss lady had said she wanted her sketch pad. Ira smiled and began to cover the cemetery a few feet at a time, gathering every single piece of paper he could find. After all, it paid the same and the basement could wait. Alice would have her sketch pad. Every single sodden scrap of it.

She was still sitting on the porch at dusk when Ira came sauntering up into the yard, his right arm piled with trash, his left hand holding it tight.

"Where in the devil have you been?"

"Just doin' my job, boss lady. You said for me to find your sketch pad so I did. Here it is. Now if the boss lady is satisfied with my efforts, I think I'll go clean up for supper and call it a day."

She stared bewildered at the muddy mess he laid in her lap. "You are an idiot."

"Now, that would be pot calling the kettle black, wouldn't it? Do with it whatever you want. Like you said, whatever you tell me to do, it all pays the same. Nice day out in the sunshine rather than staying in that damp old basement." He grinned.

She threw the soggy paper at him and crutched into the house, flames all but shooting out her ears. She'd get even, by golly she would, and he'd wish he was anywhere in the world but Huttig, Arkansas, in the Black Swan Hotel before she was finished.

CHAPTER EIGHT

Fog hugged the ground like pale gray confused clouds, not knowing that they belonged in the sky instead of hovering about the earth. The air was too warm for early September and the sun tried desperately to heat it up even more, but dark clouds kept shifting across the sky. Pine trees grew out of the fog as if their roots weren't in the rich dirt of southern Arkansas but rather in the whimsical gray matter swirling about in lazy motion.

The whole scene intrigued Alice and she tried desperately to capture the essence and symbolism of it on a canvas she'd set up on an easel out on the front porch. She hurriedly sketched it in with a pencil before picking up the palette. She needed a focal point. Something to draw the eye toward a positive idea. Three lovely Shasta daisies blooming near the porch captured her eye.

"Perfect," she said. She brushed in the

rough idea and liked the way they looked in the foreground. Subtle white with bright yellow centers and dark green foliage against the gray fog. Something as small as a daisy plant rooted and grounded while the magnificence of a tall pine tree had only shifting fog to sink its life into. She couldn't quite grasp just what it all could symbolize but it appealed to her as she painted and hummed. Occasionally she cleaned the brush across her once-white canvas painter's jacket, leaving a new color on the fabric. She was barefoot that morning, her sprained ankle turning dull yellow and green in the final stages of healing. A pair of faded, patched overall legs began where the painter's jacket ended at midthigh. Her hair had started out braided and looped around her head, but one strand had already found its way down her back and the other wasn't far behind. A smear of white began at the edge of her nose and feathered across her cheekbone like war paint on an Indian brave.

"Aren't you in a good mood for such a dreary day," Bridget waddled out to sit beside her. She wore a blue checkered smock that had about reached its stretching point. Her strawberry blond hair was done up neatly in a bun at the nape of her neck. She looked tired of being pregnant, walked like she was tired of being pregnant, sighed as she eased down into a chair.

Alice didn't look up from the canvas. "Don't ruin it. It's a lovely day. Look at those daisies."

"How's the foot?" Bridget changed the subject. Since the accident Alice had been temperamental. Before she had been quiet and content with her painting, didn't give a hoot what people thought of her, even laughed at them for thinking she was simple-minded. But the after Alice was a different person — still caring and kind but much more prone to speak her mind.

Catherine had always spoken her mind but there had been a change after Quincy came into their lives last spring. Catherine had gotten edgy, like Alice was these days. Catherine had gotten snappy, like Alice was these days. Maybe Catherine was right. Either Alice did have hidden feelings for Ira or she was ready for marriage to someone. Bridget just hoped it wasn't a sorry scoundrel like Ralph.

Bridget shuddered. Alice didn't understand just how slick men could be. Ralph was so attentive, kind, caring and sweet before their marriage but the minute she promised to love him, obey him, honor him until death parted them, it all did a hundred-and-eighty-degree turnabout. Bridget had honored and obeyed him right up until twenty-four hours before death parted them. Looking back she wasn't so sure she'd ever loved him, not after seeing Catherine with Quincy and talking to her sisters about passion.

She made a vow right then that if a man ever hurt Alice she wouldn't miss when she aimed her mother's little gun. She'd shoot him right between the eyes and then she'd help Alice bury the sorry piece of trash. It had been Alice who'd kept a cool head when Ralph died and Alice who'd sent her and Catherine home while she finished filling in the grave. People could say what they wanted about Alice, but Bridget knew beyond a doubt that night that her sister was not simple-minded. And that she had nerves of steel.

"You are frowning. Is it time for the baby?" Alice asked.

"No, not yet. But I wish it was. I'm tired of being as big as a barn and waddling like a duck." Bridget pushed the past away and managed a smile.

"It'll be here this week," Alice said.

"What makes you so sure?"

"I don't know why I know. I just do. Chalk it up to the Irish fairies that dance in my head. Poppa always said I had the biggest dose of Irish mysticism of us all. Guess it's because I'm the air daughter," she said.

"Nothing up there between your ears but air," Bridget teased.

"Hey, you don't get to give me grief. You are the water kid. That's not a whole lot more stable, you know. Pour out a glassful and see where it goes."

"Yes, but without it, the whole world would dry up and die. I'm needed whether you and Miss Earth admit it or not," Bridget said. "Answer a question for me?"

"You can ask. I might answer. I might not."

"Are you . . . Do you . . . Have you got an idea you are ready for marriage?" Bridget finally asked the question in a fast rush of words.

"Now what brought that on? I expect it would take two people to make a marriage whether I was ready or not, and I don't see a line of eligible men knocking down the Black Swan door to get at my hand," Alice said.

"Baxter has been flirting with you all this week now, and there's Ira . . . ," Bridget said.

"Ira is like a brother. Baxter would flirt with a butterfly if he thought it was female,"

Alice said.

"Watch him. His eyes remind me of Ralph," Bridget whispered.

"Who? Ira?"

"No, the other one, and speaking of the devil . . ."

"Hello, ladies. A dreary day isn't it? My, Alice, whatever can you be painting on a day like this? Wait until the sun shines and paint something cheery." Baxter leaned over her shoulder, deliberately exhaling on the tender skin right under her ear.

His breath smelled of the tobacco he rolled into cigarette paper and smoked all day. He'd shaved that morning and used some kind of nice lotion afterward, and he'd bathed the night before but his shirt had a faint odor of sourness like maybe it had picked up the aftereffects of a dirty one in the suitcase. Her nose twitched and she fought the urge to swat at him like she would a fly crawling on her neck.

"All of life is not happy, happy. There are sad times and gray times when things aren't sad or happy. Just foggy like today." She bent toward the canvas and inhaled the fresh aroma of paint.

He moved away and sat on the porch, leaning against the post and stretching his legs out in front of him. He would need new shoes by the end of the month and his socks had holes in them. He'd been rationing his tobacco. There should be enough to make it one more week. Thank goodness Catherine had left it up to him to pay the rent on the room and his dining room bill when he left because he had two quarters in his pocket and a train ticket to Memphis in his suitcase. The ticket could be changed to go most anywhere that didn't exceed the same mileage, but he'd go hungry until he got there or else he'd have to pull one slick con to get some woman to pay for his food. "But if you were happily engaged or married to the right man, then every day would be a ray of sunshine, wouldn't it?"

"Anyone who goes into a marriage thinking that has rocks for brains," Bridget said.

Baxter ignored the barb. Bridget would be the first to go when he took over the management of the hotel. Catherine wouldn't be there but a few times a year so he would only have to put on a false front for her occasionally. But Bridget with her sarcasm and the way she looked at him . . . well, she had to go. As rich as they were, she could well afford her own home and could raise her brat of a kid away from the hotel. Already the place was losing business because of the reputation Bridget had brought back to town. That crazy mixed-up story about her husband running away. She probably did kill him and hauled his body out to the river and made catfish food out of it. Baxter really didn't care what had happened but he'd be danged if he let her ruin his hotel.

"Have you been flirting with me?" Alice asked so bluntly that Baxter gasped.

The sun peeked out from behind a cloud and burned off a few more gallons of fog. The daisies stood up taller as if telling Alice they were still there and were being very still; to paint them and not ask such foolish questions.

"Yes, I have," Baxter whispered in his sexiest voice. The one that turned most women's knees to jelly and put visions of wedding cakes in their eyes.

"Are you aware that I'm the village idiot?"

"Oh, honey, I'm just aware of that little sprinkling of freckles across your nose that makes you so adorable. And I don't agree with this notion that you are simple. I think you are a . . ." Suddenly words failed him under the hot glare of Bridget's stare.

"A what? I'm listening," Alice said.

"A lovely, sweet lady," Baxter finished.

"Did you hear that, Bridget? This man thinks I'm lovely and sweet. What else could a woman want in a suitor? He's said he's flirting and now he's paying me compliments. When my foot is healed, I bet he asks me for a date," Alice teased.

"I bet he does." Baxter grinned, back on familiar ground. "Maybe if you'd allow him to drive your automobile, he would take you for a drive to get you out this afternoon."

Ira appeared like a ghost from the depths of the fog and propped a hip on the porch railing. "I've been to the lumber yard and ordered flooring for the basement. I've got the plaster up and shelving to hold your canned goods. Which reminds me, do you want the garden plowed under and the fall crops put in this week? Turnips, beets, and a new crop of potatoes?"

"That would be good," Alice said.

Ira moved behind her and leaned forward. "What are you working on? That is lovely, Alice. You've captured the fog holding down the trees and the daisies pushing the fog away. You are quite an artist. You really should think about going to the big city and putting some of your work in a gallery."

His breath was hot against her neck, sending shivers all the way to her toes. It wasn't fair. The one man who made her ache for the want of him thought she was his younger sister; the one who she could scarcely abide had all but proposed.

"Thank you, Ira, but painting is just a passing fancy of mine." Alice put the brush aside so he wouldn't see the tremble in her hands.

"As well it should be. There will come a time when you have a family and duties that are more important than playing with paint," Baxter said. That should give her something to think about, knowing that he was interested in something with more future than her little painting hobby.

"Nothing is more important than your dreams," Ira whispered so low that only Alice heard it.

"You know, I think I will take you up on that offer of a drive, Baxter. I'm about to go stir-crazy in this hotel. I'm used to being out and around and I've been cooped up here most of the week. Ira, go ahead with the garden before you start on the basement floor. You can work inside when the weather is bad." She cleaned the brush in a jar of paint thinner. "This can wait until later. After all, there are more important things than trying to mix the right shade of gray for fog, aren't there?"

It was like taking candy from a helpless baby, Baxter thought as he stood up and handed Alice her crutches. The rich little heiress would never know what hit her, quite literally if she didn't obey him. His father had taught him how to keep a woman in line. His mother died when his angry father had pushed her off the front porch during a beating. The day after she was buried, he promptly went out and found another wife. She didn't fare much better but she was still living on their crop-sharing farm south of Memphis. So what if Alice didn't live to be an old woman; there were plenty of others who would be mighty pleased to take up with a hotel owner.

Alice knew exactly what she was doing. She'd show Ira McNewel that she was a woman, not a little sister, and at the same time she'd figure out something she'd been wondering about for a long time. She went into the hotel, washed the paint from her hands and face, pinned up her hair, and put on both her shoes, even if she did tie the one on her hurt foot loosely.

Baxter waited on the porch under Bridget's hot glare. Let her try to fry him with her looks; her time was limited. When Alice came back he assisted her down the steps and into the Ford, and swaggered around the hood to the driver's side.

Alice watched him carefully. Bridget was right. There was something in his eyes that did remind her of Ralph, but he'd do for what she had in mind. After all, she didn't plan to kiss his eyes.

He gave her his brightest smile. "Where to, my lady? I am totally at your service."

"Let's drive down to the river. It's quiet there and I love the smell of the water," she said.

Baxter nodded.

Alice just proved that she was as simple-minded as everyone said. Any other woman would have wanted to go to the general store and shop, then go to the dining room at the Commercial for coffee or tea and a piece of pie. That way the whole town would see her with an eligible bachelor and know that she had staked a claim. But not Alice. She wanted to go to the river and smell the rotten old fishy water.

Baxter had had enough of that smell to last him five lifetimes. To the river at the backside of the plantation where his family sharecropped was where he had run when his father got a spell and grabbed the razor strop from the nail beside the kitchen door. Sometimes he'd lain on the black dirt banks of the water all night and until his stomach drove him back home the next day. He would have rather been bored to distraction beside a dress rack than go to the river. But it was a small price to pay for a hotel and it didn't have to be all day. He could ease his way out of that situation with a few well-placed kisses.

"Where should I park? And do you want to get out? I could carry you so you wouldn't have to use those crutches," Baxter asked as they drove down the well-worn pathway toward the water's edge.

"Park here. Yes, I do want to get out. And no, I don't want you to carry me." She pushed the door open as soon as he killed the engine.

He raced around the back of the vehicle to help her out and hand her the crutches. She deliberately dropped one and fell against him. Grasping the moment he embraced her, hugging her close to his chest, using his fist to lift her chin and never blinking as he looked deeply into her eyes.

He leaned down.

She tiptoed on her good leg.

The kiss was just as she expected — nothing earth-shattering. Not a single tingle. When it ended, she felt more like she'd just licked the bottom of an ashtray than experienced some huge rite of passage into real womanhood.

"That was very, very nice," he murmured in her ear.

She moved away. It was absolutely nothing like what had happened when Ira whispered in her ear not even an hour before. Not one bit. She had positive proof, an answer to what had been worrying her for days.

Baxter reached down and handed her the crutch. "Alice, I'm very taken with you. My heart aches to be around you all the time."

And I have wings and a halo and I'm as smart as Catherine and as lovely as Bridget.

"Shall we walk to the river and sit for a spell? Maybe I'll steal another kiss," he flirted.

"I'm ready to go back to the hotel now," she said.

"Please don't be mad at me for the kiss. I couldn't help myself. I've been smitten by you since the first time I laid eyes on you," he said.

Then why did you send Catherine those cute little postcards last spring with all that flowery language? You had seen me by then. Don't lie to me, Baxter.

"Just take me home."

"Alice, I'm going out on a limb here. It's hard to get time with you all alone. I know we haven't known each other long but I've fallen for you. I thought I was in love with Catherine but I didn't really see you until I came back to Huttig this time. Catherine was so forceful, I guess I got taken up with that. But you are like a fresh rose kissed by the dew." He paused. That line had never, ever failed him. Not one single, solitary time.

And you are the biggest liar this side of the Mississippi.

"This dew-kissed rose needs to go home right now. Did you realize there's not a single outhouse in this area?"

Baxter blushed. He would have his work cut out for him. Training the village idiot would be a difficult job but he was just the man to do it. He started the engine and backed the car around to head back to the hotel. He had about ten minutes to take advantage of a situation he might never have again so he sucked up a lungful of air. He could charm the hair off a bullfrog. Plain, freckled, simple Alice didn't stand a chance.

"Alice, I mean it. I've fallen for you. Will you marry me?" he asked.

Fallen for me. Not once have you said you love me. You do have a way with words just like old Ralph did.

"Ask me tomorrow. Right now I just want to get home in a hurry. Ask me at ten o'clock in the morning on the front porch. I'll know by then."

She was certainly living up to what everyone in town said about her.

He'd never been answered like that before. Not either time he'd been married.

"Then I shall hold my breath until that time," he said as he parked the car.

"Don't hold your breath that long. You'd look like a corpse in that shade of blue," she yelled from the porch just before she went inside.

Such indecency! He'd have to start from scratch to teach her a lady's manners. After all, he couldn't have his wife acting like that when he stepped up into the polite society of Huttig, Arkansas.

"Dang it all." He slapped the fender of the Ford, then immediately checked to be sure he hadn't dented it. After all, he liked his possessions in perfect condition.

CHAPTER NINE

"What are you doing back so soon?" Bridget asked when Alice threw her crutches on the floor and fell back on her bed.

"I didn't intend to be gone long. I wanted him to take me for a ride so I could kiss him. I did and then I was ready to come home," Alice informed her with less emotion than if she'd been discussing the foggy weather.

"You did what? The whole world is going stark raving mad. I swear, Alice, that hit on your head has affected you. I think we need to call in one of those specialists from El Dorado or maybe take you to Little Rock for evaluation."

"I've never had a clearer mind than right now. I'm going to kiss Ira next. This afternoon after lunchtime, I'm going to corner him and kiss him. Then tomorrow morning when Baxter proposes to me, I'll know whether to say yes or no," Alice told her.

"Oh, my dear God, you can not marry that man. He's evil just like Ralph," Bridget said.

"The decision isn't made yet. I still have to kiss Ira and it won't be as easy as getting a kiss from Baxter. He thinks he's some kind of special lady's man sent down here from God just to make the women swoon."

"This is crazy," Bridget said.

"Probably, but I'm going to do it. I have to so I can make up my mind. I may never get another chance at a husband and I do want to know what all the fuss is about. You didn't like marriage. Catherine loves it. So one of you knocks out the other's vote in the matter. I want to know for myself what it's like to have a husband. Someone to share a bed and talk to. Someone to sit beside me in church and hold my hand when we sit on the porch. I'm not real sure though until I kiss Ira."

"Are you in love with Ira McNewel? Catherine said you might be, but I didn't think you were so stupid as to fall for any man after the way Ralph treated me. I would've figured that would have soured you and Catherine both on marriage."

"Not me. I always planned on a husband and children. I want to be a mother. I just never figured any of the men around here would give me a chance with the reputation I have. I'm actually even jealous of you when you walk like a duck," Alice said.

"I do not walk like a duck! And why do you have to kiss Ira before you make up your mind?"

"I just do."

"Please don't marry Baxter. I'm afraid for you if you do," Bridget pleaded.

"Will you help me bury him if he hits me?"

"I'll do the honors by myself," Bridget declared.

Alice sat up, swung her legs over the bed, and reclaimed her crutches. "Don't worry, I know what I'm doing. You worry about having a baby. I'll worry about a husband."

Dottie had just returned from a walk when she saw Alice make a dash for the hotel. She didn't even give that nice man time to hold the door for her, but then Alice wasn't known for her tact or ladylike manners. None of those O'Shea women were, not these days. Her aunt Mabel said that when Ella and Patrick, their parents, were living, things were different at the hotel, but since the flu claimed them, the O'Shea girls had gone crazy. They'd always known Alice only had half a brain but after that incident with Ralph's disappearance things had gone to hell in a handbasket, according to Mabel.

Dottie wandered close to the fence separating Mabel's house and yard from that of the Black Swan. "Alice all right?" she called out to the bewildered-looking handsome man.

"I think so," he said and strolled over to the fence. "And you are?"

"Dottie. My aunt Mabel lives here. I stayed in the hotel for a few days when I first came to town but Aunt Mabel insisted I live with her until I'm ready to leave. Truth be told I'm getting homesick," she said.

He held out his hand. "I'm Baxter Wright."

Dottie was a pretty lady even if she was a little heavier than he liked his women. Dark brown hair, light brown eyes, and a ready smile, but she appeared to have all her senses about her.

"Nice to meet you, Mr. Wright. I'd be careful if I was you, staying in that hotel. They're all touched, if you know what I mean. It has something to do with the disappearance of Bridget's husband. A detective came to investigate but he got tangled up with Catherine. They say she's an Irish witch and she put a spell on him so he wouldn't find Ralph's body. I can tell you there's strange things going on in that place, so you be very careful."

"What about Ira? No one has put a hex on him." Baxter smiled.

"Well, that's because he's touched too." Dottie touched her forehead with her finger. "He's Irish and Mabel says that near-death thing he had in the Army made him crazy as they are."

Baxter listened with half an ear. "Hmmmm."

"And Alice is the worst one of the lot. She's been allowed to run all over town unsupervised since she was a little kid. Aunt Mabel says there's no tellin' what all she's done behind the bushes, if you know what I mean." Dottie's eyes shifted toward the house as if she expected to see three black witches descend upon her.

"And Bridget?" Baxter asked.

"She's the one with the horrible reputation. Catherine has powers, Alice is touched, and Bridget is a hussy. A real one. She divorced her husband and took back her maiden name and now that poor little baby is going to be born a bastard." Dottie blushed.

"But they are all rich women, right?" Baxter asked.

Dottie giggled behind her hand. "Who told you that lie? Alice or Bridget? Catherine might be rich but only if her husband,

Quincy Massey, has money. Them other two, oh, if they told you a lie like that, then they should be punished. They barely do get by. What with the Black Swan getting a bad name and no one staying there, it's been said they might have to close the doors before long. No, they're not one bit rich. Aunt Mabel says they're going to be hurtin' for money before long."

Baxter rubbed his jawline. Great God, what had he gotten himself into?

"I suppose I'd better get on inside," Dottie lingered.

"Now why would you do that? I'm enjoying our getting to know each other. You are as lovely as a fresh red rose kissed by the dew," he said.

She all but swooned.

At least he hadn't lost his touch. He'd begun to doubt it when Alice didn't respond the right way.

"Oh, you flatter me," she said with a hand over her heart and the other one pushing back a brown curl from her downcast eyes.

"Not at all. I'm just saying what I see. You said you are homesick. Where do you live?"

"I grew up in Rolla, Missouri. Poppa has a hardware store there and I couldn't bear to be tied to that store so he and Momma let me do a bit of traveling. I was on my way to Louisiana to visit a cousin but stopped off here to see Aunt Mabel. We got along fine so I'm staying with her. But I just today got a letter. Poppa is ailing and Momma's having trouble keeping the store going and taking care of him, so I suppose I should go on home," she said.

"Couldn't your brothers or sisters take care of it?" he asked. Perhaps he'd just fallen into a bed of rose petals.

"I'm an only child so no, I'll have to get on the train and go back. But you know something, after being away, it doesn't look so bad or so confining anymore. Actually, I'm kind of looking forward to going home."

He reached across the fence and touched her hand very gently. "Someone as pretty as you has a beau waiting, I'm sure."

"No, actually not. I thought I might meet someone on this trip. I don't know why I'm telling you this. I only just met you, Mr. Wright, and here I am pouring my heart out to you."

"You are so right. We have only just met but fate might have caused us to meet each other at this very moment, Miss Dottie. You see, I'm on my way to Missouri, also. I'd thought I might leave tomorrow morning on the first train north. If you'd be riding that train then we could perhaps sit together

140

and get to know each other a bit. I'm well acquainted with a hardware store. Grew up in one. My father had one in Memphis before he died. I'd be glad to escort you home and help out until your father is better."

"What a generous offer but I couldn't accept it. I've only just met you and . . ." Scarlet rose in splotches on her face.

"And if we find we don't like each other on the trip, I shall keep riding on to the northern parts of Missouri where I'm going to look at buying a small general store. If we do, then by the time we reach your home, we shall have made a new friendship. Shall we give it a try? I'm an honest, hardworking man who is lucky to have met you here this day," he said.

"What time does that train leave?"

"Seven o'clock, I do believe," he said.

"I'll be there." She smiled.

Ira stomped the spade into the damp earth again and again, not sure why he was so angry. He'd been feeling fine until he got back from the lumber yard where he'd ordered the planks for the flooring in the basement. That's when it all went to the devil on a silver poker. Alice had been painting and this morning's work was even more spectacular than any of her other pictures. The trees rising up out of the gray fog and those little daisies at the bottom of the canvas spoke to his soul. If he had the money he would offer her a handsome sum for that picture. But Ira McNewel would never have the kind of income, much less the kind of home, that would do justice to such art.

He turned the dirt over and broke up the heavy clods so that planting would be easier. That Baxter Wright was a slick character, asking to take Alice for a drive in her own Ford. Ira would have been embarrassed to ask to drive her car. She should have a suitor with his own car and it should be one of those new Buicks, one with all the chrome and every other impressive gadget that could be bought for it. She deserved the best, not a con artist like Baxter. But women were often nearsighted when it came to slick-talking men. Look what happened to Bridget and what it got her. Why didn't Alice take a lesson from that?

He was pondering that question when she let the back door slam with enough force to startle him. He looked up from his gardening, through the leftovers of fog to see her lay her crutches on the porch and settle into a comfortable place on the steps.

"I can do this job without supervision," he said.

"I know that."

"Why aren't you out letting Baxter court you?"

"What do you care?"

Ira leaned on the shovel for a moment. "Don't settle for second best, Alice. You have real talent with the paintbrushes. You could be a famous artist if you just got your pictures to the right people."

"I don't really care about being famous. I want a life, Ira."

"You have one. Right here. Huttig is a fine town and you've got the hotel and sisters who love you."

"I want a husband. I want kids. Who's going to give me that in Huttig? Any man who came courtin' would be the laughing stock of the whole of Union County."

He went back to digging. "Baxter isn't right for you."

"Come here and sit beside me for a minute," she said.

"Is that an order from the boss lady or a request from a friend?"

Friend? I guess that's better than a little sister, but not a whole heck of a lot.

"It's a request," she said.

He laid the shovel out beside her crutches

and sat down, his shoulder a good foot away from hers. Touching her was like setting his skin on fire and he had no intentions of putting himself through even more misery than he had to.

"I'll be glad when I can go down to the basement and see what you've done," she said.

"Want me to carry you down there? I've left the outside door open. It wouldn't be any trouble," he said, then wished he could recall the words. If she said no, he'd feel like he was less a man than Baxter who she'd agreed readily to go with on a drive. If she said yes, he'd have to feel her skin against his, feel her heart beating close to his own. And the pain of wanting her would engulf him again.

She raised her arms. "I'd love to see it if it's not too much trouble."

He swooped her up like he'd done at the cemetery, only this time her hair smelled of lavender and she wrapped her arms around his neck for support. He bit back the groan and willed his heart to stop racing. She was all curves and pretty red hair and cute freckles and he wanted to kiss her. But a man didn't kiss his boss lady or his friend. He kissed his sweetheart and that was something Alice could never be.

He set her down in the basement. The walls had been lathed, covered with cheesecloth, and plastered, and were as white as snow and smooth as silk. The shelves were smooth and ready to hold jars of their canning. The workmanship was exquisite but she wasn't interested in seeing Ira's handiwork. She'd known before she saw the basement it would be perfect because Ira didn't do anything halfway.

"So?" he asked.

"It's lovely. The floor will really set it off. I'm glad to get it done. Even if we aren't running at full capacity these days and could probably turn one of the bedrooms into storage, I still like this. You've done a fine job," she said and deliberately set her sore foot down on the dirt floor. She winced and fell against him.

He grabbed her in a fierce embrace. "Are you hurt?"

She wrapped her arms around his neck, tangled her fingers in his hair, and pulled his mouth toward hers. Just before his lips found hers she shut her eyes and there it was: fireworks. Red. Blue. Purple. Green. Gorgeous colors too vivid to capture on canvas because they would be so surreal. And the music, like the soft strands of a country fiddle being carried by the wind, sweeping through the tree branches beside the river.

He broke away and apologized stiffly, carried her back to the porch, picked up his shovel, and went back to work. The kiss had been exactly what he'd expected. Too intense and sweet for words. Christmas couldn't come fast enough. He needed to get out of Huttig and never look back. There would be the yearning but he could handle it if he was in another state and not staring at her across the table from him every morning at breakfast.

She picked up her crutches and went back inside.

"You are glowing," Bridget said.

"I kissed Ira. I'm going to marry Baxter. I'll tell him in the morning and we will get married by the end of the week," Alice said in a voice so flat it went below sea level.

"Why? It's plain that you liked kissing Ira," Bridget said.

"Yes, I did. It was everything I thought it would be. The most wonderful experience I've ever had in my life. But if he ever raised a hand to hit me, I couldn't shoot him, Bridget. I could never harm a single hair on that man's head, I love him so dang much. So he can't be my husband. Baxter can. Because if he ever hit me like Ralph did you,

146

I could shoot him and never think twice about it. So I'm marrying him. I want a husband and a baby. Baxter can do that for me."

"Those are all the wrong reasons to get married. Talk to Catherine. She's in love with Quincy and he doesn't hit her," Bridget pleaded.

"Families only get one miracle. Ours already got it when Catherine found Quincy. I'm not going to find a husband from Huttig and Baxter is probably the only chance I'll ever get."

"Any man is not better than no man," Bridget said.

"Good advice and I'll think on it. I've got until ten o'clock tomorrow morning to make up my mind. I just know that whether I marry Baxter or not, I can't ever marry Ira. I love him too much. He could run roughshod over me anytime he wanted. All he'd have to do would be to kiss me and I'd melt in a puddle at his feet. If I'd been standing up when he kissed me, my knees would have let me down, I swear."

"So Catherine is right. There are men out there who can make you feel all passionate," Bridget said.

"Much as I hate to give her the credit, I believe she is. If Quincy affects her that way, it's a wonder to me that she's staying with us these two weeks. If I had Ira, I'd never let him out of my sight."

CHAPTER TEN

Ira awoke before sunrise like he did every morning. He stretched his lanky frame, reaching for the ceiling. He sat down in the rocking chair and did the exercises the doctor had suggested for his leg, and then went about getting dressed. It was going to be awkward facing Alice at breakfast but it had to be done. Putting it off would just make it even stranger.

He touched his lips to see if they were still warm after dreaming about her all night. They weren't and that surprised him. She'd fit so well in his arms and kissing her had been wonderful. Actually, it had been all the things that kissing Catherine those few times had not been. With Catherine it had been pleasant; with Alice it was as if the world caught on fire.

After he'd shaved and dressed in his paint-spattered clothing he headed down to the lobby. It would be at least an hour before the ladies arose, but that would give him time to sit on the porch and plan his day. After breakfast he planned to finish planting the fall garden, then he'd go to work in the basement. In a week he'd have that job completed and then he'd start on repairing the toolshed. Alice had been right when she said she could probably keep him busy until Christmas. It seemed like every day he made up his mind it would be his last and then changed it before the next morning. But come December he was definitely leaving so he could spend the holidays with his grandparents in Mississippi. The one thing he'd missed sorely during the time he was laid up in the hospital was family during the holidays. Few of the other patients had relatives come visit that far from home, but they did have mail. Ira had none of it and he promised himself when he was discharged that he'd never spend another Christmas without kith and kin surrounding him.

He'd chosen a rocker in the far corner of the porch and stopped the movement of the chair when he saw Dottie all but tiptoeing down the road in front of the hotel. She carried a suitcase with one hand and held her hat on with the other to keep the brisk morning breeze from blowing it back to

Mabel's house.

Evidently she'd had all she could handle of her dear aunt's meddling and gossiping ways and was about to get the heck out of Huttig. She slowed down in front of the hotel and looked wistfully at the front door. She stared right at him and Ira shrunk back into the chair, trying to blend into the shadows. He didn't even want to tell the woman good-bye and good riddance for the way she'd treated Alice. Just let her get her rude self on out of town and he'd be a much happier man.

As if she willed it, the hotel door opened and Baxter Wright stepped out. He wore a suit with a nice hat set at a side angle and he carried a suitcase. Dottie smiled brightly when he joined her and she kept pace beside him as they walked toward town.

"Hmmmn." Ira rubbed his jaw. So old Baxter had been flirting around on both sides of the fence. Taking Alice out for a drive and all but telling the whole town he was interested in paying court to her and at the same time putting a smile on Dottie's face. How did he do it? Ira could barely keep up with the emotions of falling for Alice. He couldn't imagine trying to sort out his feelings among more than one woman.

"He's a worthless fool," Ira muttered.

"I'm glad he's gone but Dottie isn't half the woman Alice is, and he's an idiot for choosing her. She'll smother him plumb to death and he'll wish he was back in the war before they're together a single year."

But I'm glad he's gone. He wasn't good enough for Alice. Had shifty eyes and he didn't tell the truth. I can spot a liar a mile away in a blinding snowstorm and Baxter Wright wouldn't know the truth if it jumped up and bit him right on the hind end. Yes, sir, I'm glad he's off to other towns to work his cons. That's what he is, a con man. I bet Alice isn't the first woman he's tried to get next to. I ran into men like that in the service. Those who'd talk a lady out of her money or her underpants and then brag about it.

The sun was an orange ball back behind the trees when Sadie slipped through the hedge separating her sister's house from the hotel. She hurried into the hotel, through the lobby, and into the kitchen like she did every morning. She wore a plain yellow sprigged cotton dress that morning and her hair was done up nicely. She'd be a woman to keep a spotless house and raise a yard full of kids with a loving heart. So why couldn't Ira look at her the same way he did Alice?

He shook his head trying to get an answer.

None came out of the pine trees to land before him. Finally, he heard Catherine and Alice in the lobby and went inside to get past that first moment when he and Alice had to share space. He hoped Alice wasn't smitten by Baxter, but surely that wasn't possible. She couldn't be in love with Baxter and have kissed Ira so passionately the day before.

"Good morning," he said cheerfully when both ladies looked up from behind the desk.

Catherine was dressed in a simple work dress of blue chambray with a white collar edged in lace and white pearl buttons down to the waist. The white cuffs of three-quarter sleeves were turned up with matching buttons. A red bow knotted perfectly with even streamers was tied around her neck.

Alice wore blue-and-white-striped overalls and a white blouse with a round collar she'd left open at the neck. She was barefoot and her hair was braided in one long rope down her back. Her eyes were still puffy from sleep. Ira thought she was the most beautiful woman he'd ever laid eyes on.

"Good morning," Catherine said.

"Ira." Alice nodded.

"I smell ham frying. Sadie's already busy in the kitchen. You'll never guess what I just saw. Dottie slipping out of Mabel's house with a suitcase in her hand. Guess she's had enough of Huttig and is on her way somewhere else."

"Finally." Alice smiled at him.

His heart did a couple of flip-flops and then settled back down to normal.

"What is this with you and her?" Catherine asked.

Alice told the story of how she'd been so judgmental and had stormed out of the hotel in a snit with her aunt. "And she's snubbed me every day since. If I see her out on the porch she sticks her nose up so high in the air that she'd drown in a drizzle. If she's in the store when I go in there she acts like I'm some kind of trash."

"Well, then good riddance to bad rubbage," Catherine said. "Y'all ready for breakfast? Wonder where Baxter is? He's usually already in the dining room by now."

"He's probably sweating it out until ten o'clock," Alice said, keeping an eye on Ira.

"Why ten o'clock?" Catherine asked.

"That's when he's going to propose to me," Alice said.

She was not disappointed. Ira went an ashy gray. His mouth dropped open. Then *swoosh,* as if someone held a match to his face, he turned scarlet.

"What?" Catherine yelled. "You've got to be kidding. I won't have it. Good God, Alice, are you teasing?"

"No, he asked me yesterday but I wasn't ready to talk about it just then. So I told him to ask me again this morning at ten o'clock and I'd give him an answer," she said.

The high color left Ira's face and it turned back to a motley shade of gray, not totally unlike the fog. The color made by mixing a drop or two of pure black in with white paint. She wondered if he'd been that shade when he was mistaken for dead.

"And what is your answer?" Ira stammered.

"I haven't yet decided. I still have a few hours and I'll have to think about it some more."

"It's no," Catherine said.

"It could be yes. It's my life and my proposal. No other man in Huttig will ever propose to me. They don't want to be laughed at behind their backs for having the witless wonder for a wife. I want a husband and children. This could be my only chance."

"Ira, help me here. She's like a sister to you. Tell her Baxter is all wind and promises," Catherine pleaded.

"Baxter won't be proposing at ten o'clock. Is there money on the desk or a note from him?" Ira asked. So Alice wanted a husband and children and she didn't care who supplied them. Love didn't matter. Well, that certainly clinched it for him. He'd never commit to a woman who didn't love him with her whole heart.

"Nothing here. Why?" Catherine asked.

"And what makes you so sure he won't be proposing to me at ten o'clock?" Alice asked.

"Because he left an hour ago with his suitcase. He and Dottie were holding hands and heading toward the train station. Want me to go haul him back here?" Ira asked coldly.

Catherine shook her head. "She does not."

"Alice?" Ira asked.

"No, it's for the best, but he had no right to leave us holding the bill for a whole week's worth of room and board," she said.

Catherine wiped the back of her hand across her forehead. "It's money well lost. Now he'll never show his sorry face here again."

"Were you really going to say yes?" Ira asked.

Alice threw up her hands in a gesture of indecision. "I didn't have time to think about it so now I'll never know. I'm hungry. Let's go have breakfast."

"Good morning Sadie. Have you got enough done that I can fill a plate up for Bridget? I'm going to take her breakfast in bed this morning," Alice said cheerfully when they reached the kitchen.

Sadie pointed to a platter of fried ham, eggs, and hot biscuits.

Alice prepared a plate, picked up a napkin and silver from one of the dining room tables and left Ira and Catherine still in a confused fuddle. She didn't tell them that she was relieved to have Baxter running off with Dottie. That all night what Bridget had said about any man not being better than no man kept replaying over and over again in her head. That by morning she'd made up her mind to tell Baxter that she would not marry him and the decision had brought peace to a heart filled with turmoil. Once her mind was made up sometime around two o'clock in the morning, she'd let herself go through all the things she didn't like about the man. When she finished the list, she shut her eyes and went to sleep. It was over.

Still it did sting just a little bit that she'd taken backseat to Dottie. However, at least it wasn't Ira who'd been raked in with

Dottie's catty claws. Tightness clutched Alice's chest when that idea popped into her mind. If Dottie had talked Ira into running away with her, Alice would have had to go to the train station and rescued him, even if it meant pulling all of Dottie's hair out by the roots and scratching her eyes plumb out.

Bridget sat up in bed and rubbed her eyes. "Well, what a nice surprise. That smells like heaven."

"I'm sure the pig who gave his life so you could have this breakfast would be pleased to hear that his hind end smells like heaven," Alice said.

Bridget giggled and reached for the plate but then couldn't find a comfortable place to put it with her rotund belly in the way. "I'm going to starve before this child is born," she whined.

Alice took the plate and fixed a makeshift table for her sister. "Here, let me help. Sling your legs over the side and we'll use the wash stand for a table."

"Thank you. It tastes as good as it smells," Bridget said as she popped a bite of ham into her mouth. "I'm so ready to get things back to normal. I never knew how much I'd miss the kitchen until I couldn't go there anymore. When I get well we are going to start doing something different. I'm thinking maybe chicken pot pie on one day and chicken fried steak another. Let's think about it, huh?"

Alice changed the subject without answering Bridget concerning changing the menu. "Baxter Wright skipped out this morning without paying his bill. A whole week's worth of room plus his kitchen bill."

"That sorry piece of trash. I knew he wasn't worth anything. At least Ralph was rich and honest even if he wasn't worth a damn as a husband. He wouldn't have left us with a bill."

Alice sat down and pulled her legs up, propping her chin on her knees. "No, he'd have paid the bill and beat you black-and-blue with a belt for not ironing his shirt right."

"They're all worthless, aren't they?" Bridget asked.

"No, I think Quincy is a good man and so is Ira. Catherine is the lucky one of us," Alice answered.

"I'm glad he's gone. Were you upset? Please tell me you weren't really going to say you'd marry him."

"No, I'd made up my mind to turn him down. We might not be so lucky next time we needed a place to put a bad husband so he could push up daisies. I really think the man had his eye on the hotel more than me anyway. He had a hungry look about him, not in food hungry but for power and money."

"You are so wise, Alice. You always have been. You have the ability to see things we can't begin to understand. It must be your legacy from mother when she named you after the air. It's everywhere. It sees every-thing and knows everything. Kind of like a soft wind blowing through the trees. No one sees it but they see the effects."

"Don't be giving me credit for anything. I'm the simpleton, remember? I'll be glad when the baby gets here and Ira goes away. I'm ready for us to get back to our normal lives."

"Me too." Bridget sighed.

Catherine and Ira sat at a table together. Catherine picked at her food. She missed Quincy terribly and fully well intended to go to Little Rock the first of the next week whether the baby was born or not. Their house was ready to move into. Quincy would be back home, ready to take over his new office. A new field operative had been hired and Catherine was homesick.

"You think I should stay past Christmas?"

Ira asked.

"No, she'll be all right. She wouldn't have accepted his proposal. She's got more sense than that, Ira. I've never thought she was anything but brilliant. She's just so smart she never cared what people said. It was her inability to conform to society that started the whole thing about her not being right. Remember when she was just a little bitty girl and she would sneak off with a piece of paper and draw clouds? Well, Mabel started the whole thing. One day Alice was studying the clouds, trying to get the formations firmly in her mind. She was lying out there in the backyard, flat on her back, arms over her chest and her eyes wide open as she watched big old fluffy white clouds. Mabel told Momma that the girl wasn't right in the head. Probably had something to do with the way she was born. Actually asked Momma if she'd dropped her on her head when she was just an infant. Anyway, leave it to Mabel to start a rumor and keep it fed."

"I never thought Alice was stupid or dumb," Ira whispered.

Catherine studied his face. "That's because you thought she was going to be your little sister, right?"

"Of course it is." Ira grinned.

He fooled Catherine with his smile.
His heart didn't buy one bit of his answer.

CHAPTER ELEVEN

The preacher was sending every bootlegger to hell on a shiny silver poker and had worked his sermon around to the evils of women working outside the home. To his way of interpreting the scripture, women were supposed to be completely mindless. Little baby girls grew up to be big girls who were destined only to be wives and mothers. Woe unto the sinner who had the notion of being a doctor or a lawyer or even a hotel keeper. They were dangling by a thread no bigger than a spider's web over the flames of hell. Any moment their souls would plunge to the bottom of the pit where they would be swallowed up for their high-and-mighty ideas that went against being anything more than a dishwasher and breeding machine.

Alice listened with one ear and even that much made her more than halfway angry. She might have been ready to marry the first man who came along with a proposal, but that didn't mean she was willing to give up her soul and mind. Times had changed in the past twenty years, even more so in the past two or three since the war. Women had proven they could hold the home front down while their men left to fight, and they'd done a good job. Some had even offered their services as nurses in the effort. Did that make them all heathens and sinners? Not in the least. Alice wasn't buying that day's sermon and she wished she'd stayed home with Bridget that morning.

But nothing doing when she'd offered. Bridget had declared the baby was stuck and she was going to be pregnant for eternity. That was her punishment for hating Ralph. The only way the child was ever coming out was when it grew so big her stomach exploded. No, she would be fine, and Catherine, Alice, and Ira were going to church. The preacher would send her straight to hell if she kept one of the flock at home on the premise that the baby might arrive.

The minister slapped the podium and jerked the sleepers to attention. All eyes were on him when he lambasted divorces and the effects that such immorality would bring upon a community.

Alice glared at him.

Ira felt the force of her anger and touched her arm. She shrugged it away and stood up. He knew she was about to march up to the front of the church and give the preacher a piece of her mind. He held his breath when she made her way past him and Catherine and to the middle aisle. Several people had turned their heads to see what she was doing and the preacher lost his audience.

He slapped the podium again. It didn't get the results he wanted, so he stopped and let silence fill the sanctuary. Nothing was as scary as quiet.

Alice was about halfway to the door when he asked, "Sister Alice, where are you going?"

She turned slowly and gave him a hard look, one meant to boil him right on the spot. He didn't flinch. Neither did she.

"I asked you a question, woman. Where are you going in the middle of the sermon? Don't you know that is disrespectful?"

Catherine held her breath.

Ira bit the inside of his lip to keep from laughing out loud. The preacher had no idea what a can of wiggling worms he was about to pop open. He would do well to keep up his tirade and leave Alice alone.

"Momma told me that if I couldn't say anything nice to keep my mouth shut," Alice said loudly.

"Young lady, don't you sass me. I am a man of God."

"Then act like one," Alice said.

A hush fell over the congregation.

"Know the truth and the truth shall set you free. I have not spoken a word that is not truth."

"Good day, Reverend Cookson," Alice said.

"If you walk out that door because you think I'm wrong then you are not welcome here again, Alice O'Shea."

"Like you just said, know the truth and you shall be free. What I think of you is my business. Let your conscience be your guide, sir. And I'm not so sure I want to come back to this place. Even Jesus didn't judge and condemn the way you do."

Alice opened the back doors and stepped out into a glorious fall day. Free at last from the heat of hell's fires toasting her neck; free from a man's opinion of right and wrong. Nothing in this world was black or white. Everything was a shade of gray. There was good and bad in everyone. Her sister was not a harlot because she had divorced. The people who made moonshine didn't have horns and forked tails. Women who worked at something other than washing clothes on Monday, ironing on Tuesday, and making babies weren't sinners.

She had barely gotten into the Ford when Catherine and Ira joined her. She raised an eyebrow at her sister, who shrugged. Ira started the engine and they drove home in blessed silence.

"Just for the record, I guess the O'Sheas will have to find another church," Catherine said as they walked from the car to the Black Swan. "Look at that symbol on the door. Poppa was so proud of it and we're putting it through a mud bath."

A black circle around a silhouetted black swan with its wings uplifted had hung on the door and on the sign on the front lawn. It had been the O'Shea symbol for hundreds of years and like Catherine said, they were surely testing its patience. Ella had told them that O'Shea meant determination and integrity.

Alice removed her hat as she went into the lobby. "Well, I'd say our determination has been tested and we've passed with flying colors."

"And our integrity?" Catherine asked.

"We're standing up for our rights and what we believe in so I'd suppose it's not been dipped too much in the mud," Alice answered.

Ira cocked an ear toward the back of the lobby. "What is that noise?"

"Oh my God, it's Bridget," Alice said.

She was down to using one crutch and tried to run with it but didn't go nearly as fast as Ira and Catherine. She brought up the rear and stopped just inside the bedroom door. Bridget was lying on the floor in a puddle of water, her face shiny with sweat, her hair plastered to her head and tears rolling down her cheeks.

"Thank God you came home. It hurts. Ira, go for the doctor."

"He's on the front pew of the church," Alice said.

"I'll get him," Ira promised.

"What do we do? And why are you on the floor?" Catherine asked.

"I got up to go to the bathroom and my water broke. It hurt so bad I just sat down and then it hurt too bad to get up and back in bed. Besides, it would make a mess on the mattress. God, I want to push this baby out."

"You can't. The doctor isn't here."

Alice tossed the single crutch to the side and sat down at her feet. She threw Bridget's robe up over her mounded stomach and drew her underdrawers off. "Yes, you can. I'm right here and we can do this." She put her hand on Bridget's stomach and when the next contraction hit she said, "Okay, push with all your might."

Bridget obeyed.

"There's a little bit of its head coming out now. Push again," Alice said.

Bridget held her breath and pushed.

"Not like that. You didn't do a bit of good that time. When you hold your breath it sucks the baby back up in there. You want it out, you push, girl."

Bridget pushed.

"Okay, we've got a head out." Alice supported the baby's head and went to work cleaning the mouth and nose. "Shoulders next. Give it all you got left. It's a big baby, Bridget, and you've got to work with me."

Two minutes later, a perfectly formed chubby little girl lay on the floor screaming her head off.

"You've got a daughter. Catherine, grab her sewing basket over there and go get me some alcohol out of the bathroom," Alice barked.

Catherine was back so fast Alice couldn't believe she'd even left the room. She poured alcohol on the scissors, letting it drip right onto the hardwood floor and not even caring that it would strip the finish off. She tied off the umbilical cord with a strip of embroidery floss from the sewing kit and then cut it, took care of the placenta when it passed, putting it in a pillowcase so the doctor could check it.

Then she wrapped the new baby in the sheet she dragged off the bed and put her on Bridget's stomach. "There you go. Baby is here. Catherine, get us a pan of warm water so we can get both of them cleaned up and put to bed where they belong."

Catherine literally fell backward in a chair and turned as gray as yesterday's ashes. "My lord, where did you learn to do that?"

"Water, please?" Alice demanded.

Catherine moved.

Alice bathed her sister and dressed her in a fresh gown, underpants, a belly binder, and padding while Catherine followed orders and put fresh linen on the bed. Then they lifted Bridget onto the bed.

"Now I need more water to bathe the baby and you need a bucketful to clean up this floor," Alice said.

"Yes, ma'am," Catherine said.

When the doctor came rushing in, Alice had the squalling baby girl laid out on the wash stand, carefully washing the white film from her body. "You are a day late and a dollar short, Doc. Did the preacher have trouble letting you out too?"

"Little bit. Looks like you got it all took care of." He smiled.

"Please check the afterbirth and it might not hurt to make sure I got her taken care of," Alice said.

Catherine blushed and left the room. "I'll finish this later."

"I'm not leaving. This baby will freeze if I don't get this done," Alice said.

"You ever think of working as a nurse?" the bald-headed, overweight doctor asked.

"No, sir. I would not like that at all."

"Where'd you learn to deliver a baby?"

"It's not that much different than bringing baby kittens into the world. I knew we couldn't wait for you and it had to be done," Alice answered.

Bridget looked up with tears in her eyes. "Oh, I've ruined your church dress."

"Don't reckon I'll be needing it anytime soon, so who cares." Alice dressed the baby in a soft diaper and a gown, then wrapped her tightly in a blanket before handing her to her mother.

"Miss Ella, meet your Momma. If you grow up to be half the woman she is, you'll be doin' just fine," Alice said.

Ella mewed, not totally unlike a kitten.

171

"Hungry already?" Bridget asked.

"Everything looks fine. Couldn't have done a better job myself," the doctor pronounced. "Feed her and watch her grow. I'll be back in three days to check on both of you. You are to lift no more than her weight for ten days. Sit in a chair when you feel up to it. Walk around the bedroom at first and then the living room. By the end of the week you can go to the porch."

"I'll make her listen," Alice said.

"I don't doubt it." The doctor chuckled.

"Ain't she beautiful?" Bridget bared a breast and Ella latched right on, sucking greedily.

Alice touched the baby's head. "Black hair and green eyes."

"Oh, you can't tell about the eyes yet and her hair could turn dark red like Catherine's and Momma's."

"It's black like her father but that's the only thing she's getting from him," Alice said.

Catherine peeked inside the room. "Is it all right if Ira comes in?"

"Not just yet," Alice said. "Ella is nursing. Give her a few minutes. You come sit with her, Catherine, and I'll get cleaned up and start lunch."

■ ■ ■ ■

Ira knew exactly how an expectant father felt as he paced the floor waiting for the doctor to come out. He listened intently for a shrill cry but heard nothing and feared that Bridget had gone through the whole ordeal with nothing but a stillborn child at the end. When the doctor reappeared so quickly, he stopped his circuit from the door to the dining room archway, across to the front door, around two settees and back to the starting point.

"It's a girl. She's fine. Momma is fine. Alice would make one heck of a fine nurse. Nothing rattles her cage. If there were more women like her in the world it would be a better place," he said with a wave and left.

Ira sat down with a thud on one of the settees and didn't even hear Alice thumping across the floor. When she melted into the spot beside him he jumped. She had blood all over her pale blue church dress, her hair was escaping the pins, and her hands were shaking.

"Are you all right?" he asked.

"I'm fine. No, I'm not, but I couldn't let Bridget and Catherine see me like this. It would upset them. I don't fall apart in a crisis. I keep my head about me and do just fine, but when it's all over, I crumble. This is . . . Oh, my God, Ira, I just delivered my niece! She's beautiful and she's got black hair and what if I'd broken her neck bringing her out of Bridget or what if I'd done something wrong and hurt Bridget? Doc says I did it right but what if . . ."

He slipped his arm around her. She shook like an oak leaf in the middle of a major tornado. He pulled her close to his side, hoping that his own fears wouldn't transfer to her to make matters worse. "It's all right," he said. "Doc said you could be a nurse and nothing rattled you. You did a good job in there. Bridget got her daughter and it's all over."

"I couldn't wait for him. The baby was coming and Bridget was so tired and —"

"Shhh. Hush now," he whispered. "You can fall apart right here and no one will ever know. I won't tell."

She laid her head on his chest and listened to the steady beat of his heart. That alone began to settle her nerves, but not enough to keep the flood of tears at bay. They swept down her cheeks soaking the front of his shirt.

"Promise you won't tell Catherine I was a big baby?" she asked.

"You've got my word on it. And you aren't a big baby. You should have seen Catherine's face when she came out here. I thought she was going to faint dead away," Ira said.

"But Catherine is the brave one. I'm just a bit of thin air," she said.

"You are the bravest woman I know. You walked out on a preacher."

She managed a weak smile when the tears ceased. "And God didn't even strike me dead with a lightning bolt."

He brushed at the wet streaks on her cheeks when she looked up at him. One moment he was looking into the prettiest green eyes this side of heaven and the next he was kissing the softest lips in the whole universe.

Sparks danced.

Time ceased.

Two hearts beat in perfect unison.

She broke away and opened her eyes. Yes, it was plain old Ira McNewel. Not a prince in shining armor. "I think I'd better go on and get cleaned up now. You and I will most likely have to put dinner on and the crowd will be arriving any minute now. You can bet your bottom dollar they'll all be here today to see if God has punished me for my heathenistic ways."

Ira nodded. He couldn't have said a word if his life depended on it. Twice now he'd kissed her and the jolt of desire had glued his tongue to the roof of his mouth. It was probably best if he did leave as soon as possible. Alice O'Shea could have him wrapped so firmly around her tiny little finger that he'd be henpecked from the time he said "I do."

CHAPTER TWELVE

Rain poured in slabs as wide as the state of Arkansas and thicker than a concrete wall the morning that Alice and Ira took Catherine to the train station. They arrived with only a few minutes to spare and no time for long good-byes. Catherine hugged Ira like a brother and held on to Alice for an extra moment. Part of her wished she could stay in Huttig and watch Ella grow up but the other part wanted to go home to Little Rock and kiss her husband until neither of them could catch a breath.

"Take care of her," she said to Ira as he helped her to the train with the only available umbrella they could locate that morning at the hotel.

"Are you talking about Alice? She doesn't need anyone to take care of her. She's a rock," Ira said.

"She can be but she can be as fragile as a spring breeze too. Watch out for her, Ira,"

Catherine said.

"I'll do what I can," he promised.

Alice watched from the window of the station but she couldn't see anything but faint gray silhouettes once Ira and Catherine left the shelter of the porch roof. Things were always easier when Catherine was around. She brought peace and stability. Alice wiped at the tears and swallowed hard before Ira came back into the station, a small room with a few old oak pews probably inherited from a church. The week before when Ella had been born she'd fallen to pieces in front of him and sworn it would never happen again. She heard the train pull away, taking Catherine with it. When she looked up Ira was sitting beside her, a foot of air between them.

"Ready to go?" he asked.

"I suppose I have to," she said in a high squeaky voice.

"You could paint today. The hotel is empty and not many folks will brave this kind of weather to come out for lunch. We should have a slow day."

Before she could answer several people tried to get through the door at once. All of them wiping rain from their faces and shaking it from their clothing and hair: a gray-haired man with a big wide handlebar mustache; a lady of about the same age; two young men in their mid- to late twenties and two women spaced somewhere in that age frame.

"Excuse me, could you recommend a hotel? My family needs a place to stay for a couple of days," the man asked Ira.

"The Commercial Hotel is closest, but I work at the Black Swan. It's smaller and the food is much better. Alice O'Shea and her sister, Bridget, own the hotel and it has fine accommodations if you can make do with seven rooms. This is Alice right here," he said.

"We could make it with less but six would be nicer," he said. "And would you be able to give us transportation to the hotel?"

"I would. It will take two trips. I could take the ladies first and return for you gentlemen," Ira said.

"That would be wonderful. I am Robert Lee Levy. This is my sister, Marlee Rosenthal, and her children, Emma and Annie, and Lester and Cyrus. We are on our way from New York to New Orleans and we're very tired of the train, so we thought we'd stop over a few days for some real food and rest," he said.

"I suppose you'll have to make three trips," Marlee said. "We have quite a lot of luggage."

"I can do that," Ira said. "How many umbrellas do you have?"

Marlee shook her head. "They're packed in our baggage, I'm afraid."

"Okay, Alice and I have one so I'll take you ladies out to the car one at a time. Miz Marlee, you can be first," he said.

It wasn't easy to watch Emma and Annie hook their arms though Ira's and snuggle up entirely too close to his side under the big black umbrella, but Alice managed to keep the jealousy at bay. After all they were paying customers for the hotel and restaurant even if for a split second she had liked the idea Ira put forth about using the whole day to paint.

Sadie would have to do double duty the next few days, keeping up with the room cleaning and the cooking, but she wouldn't mind making the extra money. But then that too posed a problem. It would give her even more hours to flirt with Ira. Alice almost moaned. She couldn't win for losing.

"Your turn." Ira popped his head inside the door and looked at Alice.

When she stepped outside under the umbrella he threw an arm around her shoulders and pulled her close enough to his side that she could feel the warmth of his body through his chambray shirt. She wished she could stay there for hours and analyze each and every emotion dancing through her body like a band of gypsies around a warm fire, but all too fast he was helping her inside the Ford with the other three ladies and making his way around the hood to the driver's seat.

"I'm so excited to be off that train for a couple of days," Emma said. "I can't ride and read and it's so boring. At first the countryside entertained me but after a few hours it all began to look the same."

Alice turned in the passenger's front seat to see the women. Marlee was a stout woman with gray beginning to salt her black hair. She had a round face, lovely blue eyes, and a strong chin. She wore a navy traveling dress with sturdy shoes and an enormous diamond ring on the ring finger of her left hand.

"We'll build a fire in the lobby and you can read all day. Huttig is a very small town but you might enjoy a trip to the general store or just being able to walk around," Alice said.

"I'll just be glad to get out of these clothes and have a nice warm bath," Marlee said. "Do you have modern bathrooms?"

"Yes, ma'am. Poppa insisted on bathrooms

and telephones," Alice said.

"Then I'm calling for first rights to the bathtub. Besides I'm the mother and the oldest so I get my way," she teased.

"Momma, I haven't washed my hair in two days. You'll use all the hot water and —" Emma whined.

"And you will wait for it." Marlee pointed.

"Without pouting," Annie said.

"I can pout if I want but I won't. I'm just so happy to have a bed that isn't sitting on rolling wheels that I shall be content with my lot," Emma said stoically.

Annie giggled.

Annie had dark curly hair cut in one of the new bobbed styles. Her features looked as if they'd been set in place by the angels themselves. Dark, perfectly arched brows and long lashes framed her dark brown sparkling eyes. Her nose was just shy of being too small but no one would ever notice because she had a full bow-shaped mouth that magazine models would absolutely die for. She wore a navy skirt and a middy blouse with a red tie knotted at the sailor collar and a gold watch. No rings on her fingers so evidently she was still single.

Alice frowned. Another one to flirt with Ira. She studied Emma with side glances to see if there was even more trouble arriving at the Black Swan. Emma had the same color hair as Annie but it was longer and swept up in curls on top of her head. Her eyes, framed with dark lashes and eyebrows, were pecan colored and more pensive than her sister's. Her nose was slightly bigger and was slightly out of proportion with her lips, which were thinner and more severe. She wore a tan traveling suit with a slim skirt and matching jacket with a cream-colored silk blouse. Where Annie would flirt right out in the open like Sadie, Emma would be more discreet and sly.

Yes, Emma would bear watching as much or more than Annie. Why, oh why had Alice insisted on staying to see Catherine get on the train? Had she simply delivered her that morning and then gone right back home, these people would be staying at the Commercial because it was closer. Now she had a full hotel, a kitchen to run, and meals to prepare and a sister with a week-old baby. She'd never have the time to keep Ira safe.

Bridget was sitting in one of the easy chairs with Ella when the ladies arrived, one at a time, Marlee first. By the time Ira escorted Alice inside all three were gathered around her making baby noises. No one even noticed him go back to the train station for the rest of the guests.

183

Sadie came out of the kitchen drying her hands on the tail of her apron and raised an eyebrow at Alice. "Guests?"

Alice nodded. "Have you ladies had breakfast?"

Annie looked up. "We ate in the train car."

"Would you like some hot tea and cookies?" Sadie asked.

"That would be wonderful," Marlee said.

"I'll have it out in a few minutes. Three of you?" Sadie asked.

"Six. Three more on the way. Our uncle and brothers," Annie said.

"Then I'll put out coffee as well and extra cookies," Sadie said.

"This is so cozy and nice," Emma said. "Are our rooms upstairs?"

"Yes, and Ira will take you up when he gets back. I sprained my ankle severely and I'm just now getting around without crutches. The doctor won't let me climb stairs for a few more days," Alice explained.

"Is Ira your brother?" Emma asked.

"No, he's an old family friend who came back from the war and needed a job," Bridget answered. "It's so damp out today we'll get him to start a small fire just to take the fall chill off when he gets back. It won't stay this way, though. It's just the middle of

September so we've got lots more warm days."

"I'm going to help Sadie." Alice left Bridget to do the entertaining. She was better at it anyway and how could anyone compete with a tiny baby? Maybe that was the answer to how she'd keep Ira safe. Just keep Bridget in the lobby all the time and the ladies would be so taken up with Ella, they'd forget all about him.

By the time Ira delivered Robert and his nephews and showed them to their rooms, Sadie and Alice had laid out a table in the dining room with several kinds of cookies, coffee, and tea, and a pitcher of ice-cold milk. The guests barely took time to get their baggage into the right rooms before they were back in the dining room, filling cups and finding places to sit while they enjoyed a midmorning snack.

"Wouldn't want to sell the place, would you?" Robert asked Alice as he reached for another hand full of raisin oatmeal cookies.

"No." She shook her head emphatically.

"It's exactly what I'm looking for," Marlee said. "We were in the jewelry business in New York. Third generation. My grandparents founded the business and my father went into it when he married our mother. Then Robert and I inherited it and my late

185

husband worked with us. We sold it a couple of months ago and decided to relocate. I really want a restaurant to keep me busy and this place has enough bedrooms to house the family. And I want it where there are no hard cold winters."

"She wouldn't ever sell the Black Swan. Her father built it back when Huttig was just becoming a town," Ira said from the archway.

"And that was?" Cyrus asked.

"Sixteen years ago," Alice said.

"Ah, a brand-new town. Mother, we really should take a look at this area. It's not ancient like New York City," Cyrus said.

"We'll have to discuss it later," Marlee said. "How much would you charge me for the use of your kitchen?" she asked Alice bluntly.

"I can't rent the kitchen out. We cook every day for our patrons. The dining room is usually full at dinner and supper," Alice said.

"Then can I help the cook?" Marlee asked. "I love to cook but I've never prepared for more than fifteen people on my own. I'd love to see how a real restaurant is run."

Alice could scarcely believe her ears. "You want to work?"

"And so does Annie and Cyrus." She nodded.

Alice jerked her head around at Annie, who was also nodding.

Cyrus was grinning. "Annie and I love to cook. We're going to help Mother when she finds her own restaurant. I know it sounds like a crazy idea but we really would like to learn from your cook."

Alice looked at Emma, who raised her palms and shook her head. "Lester is more interested in writing. He was a war correspondent for the *New York Times* and has only just returned home. I don't cook. Hate it. Absolutely do not like the sight of raw eggs or even raw pancake batter. All that slime and goo. Give me a paint palette and a blank canvas any day of the week. I'll either read or sketch while they learn the fine art of making southern food."

"Don't look at me, child. I love to eat the food, not prepare it," Robert said. "I've worked forty years making and selling fine jewelry. I'm going to spend my days here walking around town and enjoying the sunshine, if it ever comes out. I am officially retired and intend to act like it."

Marlee dropped her chin and looked up at him over the top of her eyebrows. Emma and Annie snickered. Lester and Cyrus guffawed.

"That might last two days," Emma said. "And then he'll be out trying to buy a railroad or something where he can wheel and deal."

Ira slipped out of the room and went to the basement where he was still carefully building a wood floor. He picked up a jointer and ran it down the length of a board, giving it a nice even edge to fit up against the last one. It wasn't easy leaving Alice up there with two nice-looking young men who must be as rich as Midas if their uncle could buy a railroad. They'd all be lunatics if they couldn't see her beauty.

"And that Cyrus will be working in the kitchen with her," he moaned to himself.

What would happen if they did wear her down in the next couple of days and she and Bridget sold the Black Swan? He had enough money to go to Mississippi, but the thought of Alice and Bridget moving to Little Rock lay like a stone in his chest. Alice, up in Little Rock where there were even more rich men; men who didn't have any preconceived notions about her mentality. Doll her up in an evening gown and take her to a fancy party and the suitors would be stumping their toes trying to get a chance at a dance with her.

"That's what she deserves," he muttered under his breath.

Ira would simply have to get over his infatuation. He'd have to get past it and go on with his life. Whether it was two days from now when Bridget and Alice moved out of the Swan and to Little Rock to be close to Catherine or three months from now when he moved on to Mississippi, the outcome would be the same. Ira and Alice would say good-bye and it would be over. What might have been would be water under the bridge. What could have been would be past history with no hope of a future.

Even if he did marry sometime in the future, he'd always keep a corner of his heart for Alice — the woman who made his heart beat faster and who made the world stop for a minute when she kissed him. He'd visit the corner every year in the fall and remember the day she fell off the ladder and on top of him, and the memories would feed his lonely soul.

CHAPTER THIRTEEN

Marlee picked an apron off one of the nails behind the door and tied it around her ample middle section. "Now tell me what we are cooking today?"

"Chicken and dumplings, sweet carrots, hot yeast rolls, and apple pies," Sadie said. She was more than a little nervous at having three more people in the kitchen. Rich people by the looks of their dress and that ring on Mrs. Rosenthal's finger.

"How do you make chicken and dumplings? I've heard of them but never actually prepared or eaten them." Cyrus said.

"We've already got the chickens boiling. They're nearly finished." Alice stepped in to explain. "We'll take them out when they're done. When they're cooled enough to work with we'll debone and cut them into bite-size pieces and return them to the broth. Then we make dumplings out of flour, baking powder, shortening, and milk, and drop them into the boiling liquid."

"Oh, you mean chicken pot pie?" Annie said. "Only we roll the dough into strips."

"No, chicken pot pie is made with pie crust and vegetables. We're making pies today so we'll make one to show you," Sadie said.

"I'm good at hot rolls. Give me the recipe and I'll lay claim to a corner over there," Cyrus said.

He was the very one that made Sadie the most nervous. To think of a man in the kitchen with an apron hanging down to his knees was enough to bring on an incurable case of the giggles.

"And I'm good at pie crusts. I'll make the apple pies. How many?" Annie said.

"Ten ought to do it," Sadie said.

"Do you make a crust recipe at a time or all ten at once?"

"I usually make them up two at a time. Seems like the crust gets tough if you work the dough too much and that happens if you do ten at once," Alice answered.

"Make enough crust for twelve pies and we'll show you how to make a real chicken pot pie while you are at it," Sadie said.

Alice nodded approval.

"So tell me about you and your sister," Cyrus said as he worked. "You were raised up in this hotel?"

Alice opened several jars of carrots, poured them into a stockpot and added brown sugar and butter. "That's right. Poppa brought us here when we were just little girls." She went on to tell the story of how the Black Swan was the first hotel in Huttig. The Commercial came along two years later and garnered most of the company trade, as did the commissary store. But the small businesses such as the Black Swan and the general store made a healthy living so there was little competition.

"You mentioned three sisters. Where's the other one?" Cyrus asked.

He had jet-black hair he combed from a perfect side part, a dimple in his chin, and brown eyes set under heavy dark brows and lashes so thick they looked like they belonged on a girl. But even in an apron and making hot rolls there wasn't one feminine thing about Cyrus Rosenthal. He was all man and if he wore a pair of cowboy boots and spurs, his likeness could be used on the front of a dime store western novel.

"There are three of us. Catherine is married and lives in Little Rock. She left on the northbound this morning to go home. She's been with us two weeks," Alice said.

"Come see if this dough looks elastic

enough to suit you," Cyrus said.

When she got close enough he whispered, "You have the most beautiful hair and eyes."

"Thank you," she said.

"Are you seeing someone?"

"Oh, yes. I'm practically engaged. That dough looks just fine. You really do know your way around a big bowl of hot rolls, don't you?"

Now why in the world had she done a fool stupid thing like that? The man was rich, fine-looking, and could even cook, and she'd just told him a blatant lie. He didn't know her reputation for having air for brains and he was flirting, and she'd just put up a solid brick wall. She really did have an empty space between her ears where a brain was supposed to exist.

Ira shaved the side of a plank and set it in place. It was a quarter of an inch too long so he took it back up and carefully removed the excess. When he laid it back down, it fit perfectly, so he nailed it in place. He wasn't aware that anyone was in the basement with him until he picked up another board.

"Hello, Ira," Lester said. "I hope I'm not intruding. Bridget said it would be all right if I came down here. She told me a little about you being in the war and being thought dead."

"That's right," Ira said.

"Mind if I sit and talk to you while you work?"

"Not at all."

"Actually, I'd like to ask you some questions and make some notes. I'm still writing for several newspapers and magazines and I've got this idea about doing a series of stories about men coming home from the war and how their lives have changed," Lester said.

Ira stopped work and sat down in an old fiddleback kitchen chair that had been tossed in the basement when a rung broke out of the back. "What kind of questions?"

"Just questions. If they make you uncomfortable just say so and we'll go on to something else. I got the idea riding the trains. There were so many ex-soldiers looking for work or going home. I visited with them and the stories were endless. I'm considering writing some novels, also, but right now I'm just taking notes and weighing my options."

"I suppose that would be all right."

Lester flipped open a notepad and took a pencil from his vest pocket. "Were you born and raised here in Huttig?"

Ira nodded.

"Huttig is just sixteen years old. I wasn't born here but I was just a little boy when Momma and Poppa came here from Mississippi. Poppa got on at the mill. So he brought Momma and two boys and a girl and this became home."

"So when the war was over you simply came home and got a job here at the hotel. Why here?"

"Because I didn't have a dime in my pockets and the mill wasn't hiring. They'd laid off all their surplus help when the war ended. Didn't need so much when the government contracts played out."

"So did you know Alice and Bridget before you returned from the war?"

"I guess you could say that." He went on to tell Lester the story he'd told Alice earlier, ending with the fact that he'd come to see Catherine and tell her he wasn't the same man who'd gone off to the war and his feelings had changed.

"Oh, my, that is some story," Lester said. "So you plan to stay here or are you just hired on until you get the renovations finished?"

"I told Alice I'd stay until Christmas. That'll give Bridget time to get on her feet after the baby and it'll give me enough time to finish all these jobs. The hotel should be in good repair by then. I'm intendin' on going to my grandparents' in Mississippi and maybe I'll stay there. I missed the farm when we left it. But Poppa wanted to light out on his own and he never did like farming."

"Well, I'll let you get on back to your work," Lester said. "Guess I'll see you at the lunch table."

"Round here, we call it dinner. The evening meal is supper."

"Okay." Lester smiled showing off near-perfect white teeth.

His left eye tooth overlapped the one next to it but that was a small imperfection in his looks. He was shorter than Cyrus and his hair wasn't as black but he was good-looking enough to give Sadie a case of the hives, Ira figured. He just hoped Alice was off in one of her alternative worlds and wouldn't be affected by the two young Rosenthal men.

That evening after supper, Alice left the guests in the lobby talking about how much fun they'd all had that day. Marlee had decided after one day in the kitchen that she definitely wanted a restaurant somewhere in the South where it was warm and the winters were mild. Annie was busy thumbing through the Sentinel Stove Manufacturing Company cookbook Catherine had bought when it had first come out four years before. She had her head down and wrote recipes into her notebook while everyone else talked. Emma was excited because Alice had loaned her an artist easel and she had spent the day sketching Bridget holding Ella. Tomorrow she would work with her watercolors. It wouldn't be her best work but she was elated that she'd found a willing subject and an easel.

Robert declared that he'd spent a lovely day visiting with a gentleman named Major Engram and they were going fishing tomorrow. He liked Huttig and might come back there to visit but it was much too small for him to entertain notions of living there permanently. Only if Union would sell him the sawmill would he consider changing his mind.

Alice slipped through the family living room and out to the back porch. Truth be known, it had been a trying day for her. She was a self-proclaimed hermit and could abide normal guests, but these folks were like a hoard of family coming to visit. They'd been in her kitchen, talking constantly. Her ears hurt from so many words.

She needed peace and pure quiet for a while.

With a heavy sigh she eased down on the porch, leaning her back against the porch post. A soft evening breeze ruffled the pine needles ever so slightly. Fall was on the way but it would be a couple of months before summer threw in the towel and left the state. Other than the sweet cooing of a dove in the distance everything was quiet.

Then the argument began. It sifted through the trees between the hotel and house right next door. Mabel and Henry were disagreeing over something, which wasn't any surprise. They agreed on very little.

"I'm telling you she's making a big mistake. That man had shifty eyes and he'll —" Mabel was saying.

"Oh, stop your fussin', woman," Henry said. "Dottie might look all soft and sweet but she's a cougar underneath all those ruffles and done-up hair. If old Baxter thinks he's getting a woman who'll do his biddin' he's got a big surprise comin'."

"She can hold her own but he reminds me of that Ralph Contiello that Bridget married. He's liable to beat her. How'd you like that? She was like a daughter to me and you'd sit there and let a man beat her?"

"He'll beat her one time and then she'll set him straight," Henry said.

"What's going on around here?" Ira said from the corner of the house.

Alice jumped and put a finger over her mouth and whispered conspiratorially. "Shhh. Sit down and listen. It appears that Baxter and Dottie did leave together and Mabel is worried about her."

"Dottie can take care of herself," Ira said.

"That's what Henry says," Alice said.

"Did you hear voices?" Mabel said.

"No and neither did you."

"Yes, I did. Coming from over there in that hotel. It's a den of sin, I'm telling you, Henry. Two women running a business like that. Men folks up in those rooms. Just think how easy it would be for them to —"

"You are an incurable gossip. I'm going in the house to listen to the radio before they shut down the station."

Ira chuckled. "Sounds like Henry knows her pretty good. So how was your day with all those folks in your kitchen?"

"Noisy and strange. Never had guests who wanted to help cook before. How were the hot rolls?"

"Light and fluffy like always. I did like that chicken pot pie too," he said.

"Cyrus made the hot rolls and Sadie

taught Annie how to make the pie. Up there where they come from they call chicken and dumplings chicken pot pie, so Sadie was showing Annie the difference. You think we ought to put the pot pie on the menu and give folks a choice on Thursdays?"

"Might be nice," Ira said. "Y'all been talking about doing some different things. That might be the way to ease into it. Start making two main dishes and give them a choice."

"I like that idea. I'll talk to Bridget about it. You had it lucky. You got to stay in the basement away from all of them. Sometimes I wish we'd have just offered to take them to the Commercial."

"And miss out on that much money? That's not a businesswoman I hear talking. And my day wasn't a lot better than yours. Lester cornered me in the basement and wanted to hear that whole story about me being dead and why did I come back here and the whole thing."

"Why?" Alice asked.

"He's writin' some stories about the men who came home and what changed in their lives after the war. I got to thinkin' about it after he left and you know, I guess we've all got a story to tell. Maybe some of us wasn't given up for dead but there's men folks coming home to sweethearts who didn't wait, who are married to someone else. There's those like me who are coming home to parents who are gone now. It's not just me who's been given a raw deal."

"I told a lie today," she blurted out.

He looked at her sitting there in the evening light and wondered what in the world she was talking about. Had she not heard a word he said as he poured his heart out to her?

"I did," she said again.

"Okay, Alice. What did you tell a lie about?" he asked.

"Cyrus asked me if I was seeing someone and I told him I was almost engaged. So if any of them ask you, would you not tell them I'm —"

"Why did you tell him that? Those are some powerful, rich folks in there, Alice. Maybe he's interested in you," Ira said, jealousy turning his soul black even as he said the words.

"Because I'm not interested in them. They're nice people and wonderful guests but I just plain don't want to deal with them. I don't care who's powerful or rich or even who's a con artist like Baxter. Did I tell you that he proposed to me?"

Ira almost swallowed his tongue. "He did

what? What did you tell him? Was it that day he took you for a drive? Lord, Alice, he's a slick scam artist. You didn't tell him you'd marry him, did you? Surely you've got enough sense not to be taken in by the likes of him."

Her nerves bristled. "How dare you talk to me like that. I'm not your danged sister, Ira. Of all the people in the world, I never thought you'd be throwing it up in my face about having sense or not having it. I thought you knew me better than that. And no, I didn't tell him I'd marry him. I told him he'd have to come back the next morning at ten o'clock and ask again and I'd think about it. It was . . ." She clamped her mouth shut. She'd almost told him that she had to come home and kiss him before she'd consider marrying a man she didn't love.

"It was what, Alice?" Ira asked through clenched teeth. She could ruffle his feathers quicker than any woman on earth. God only knew why.

"Bridget told me any man wasn't better than no man and I thought about it all night. Even though he'd done run off with Dottie before ten o'clock the next morning, I'd already decided to tell him no, I would not marry him. So there, Ira. Are you satisfied or do I need to get some more sense before I let another man kiss me?"

"He kissed you?" Ira hissed.

"Actually I kissed him," Alice said.

"Then yes, you need to get some more sense," he said as he stood up and walked away from her.

"Men! They say women are temperamental, but they aren't anything compared to men with a burr in their shortalls," she said.

Ira turned so quickly his weak leg almost took him to the ground. "Good God, Alice. Ladies don't talk about men's underwear."

"I don't have enough sense to be a lady, remember? Maybe I ought to go in there and tell Cyrus that I just broke up with my fiancé and thank him again for telling me my hair and eyes were pretty."

Ira's eyes narrowed into mere slits. "You told him you were engaged to *me?*"

"No, I did not, and it'll be a cold day in hell before I ever am. You'll be looking for a wife with a lot of sense, not a witless wonder. Good night, Ira. I'll see you at the breakfast table." She stormed into the house.

CHAPTER FOURTEEN

Alice was so engrossed in making long strokes on the drawing paper that she didn't hear Emma walk up behind her. Two lines later she had his back muscles perfected under the tight-fitting chambray shirt; if only she could draw his face, but that had been a futile attempt for the past eight years.

"It's Ira, right?" Emma whispered.

Alice jumped and threw the charcoal pencil out in the yard. "Yes, it is," she admitted after her heart slowed down. "I can't do portraits. I'd love to but they don't come to life like yours do. Did you finish Bridget and Ella?"

"Just now. It's not my very best work but it kept me occupied a couple of days. If I hadn't gotten off that rumbling train, I think I'd have gone stark raving mad."

"How did you leave behind everything you've known your whole life?" Alice asked.

"It's a lark. Mother thinks she wants a

restaurant because she loved coming home from the jewelry business every day and making supper. It was her escape from the hectic world she lived in during the day. Uncle Robert thinks he wants to retire. Cyrus, Lester, Annie, and I needed a vacation so we came along. By the time we spend a month near the ocean we'll all be ready to go home and get back into the groove we're used to," Emma said.

"But there's no business there. What will you do?" Alice asked.

"There's no diamond business. Mother designs the most gorgeous jewelry so I expect she'll start selling her own line. Uncle Robert will find something else, probably marketing Mother's designs. Annie will find a husband and make a lovely wife. Cyrus might go on to be a chef in some fancy restaurant. Lester will continue his writing and me, well, I plan to do an art show. You should do a show too, Alice. Your stills are absolutely breathtaking. I could never do that kind of work. I'm a portrait artist. But your art has a life and breath of its own. You are really very good. I don't know why you'd ever consider portraits."

Alice couldn't tell her that the only portrait she wanted to do was Ira so that she could remember every single detail of his face and body. That she'd been infatuated with Ira since she was twelve years old and she'd probably never love another man like she did him.

"Thank you for saying that," Alice said.

"So are you just using Ira for a study since he's here or is he the man you are practically engaged to? Don't look shocked. Cyrus was quite taken with you but he said you were seeing someone else. I wish you weren't. You'd fit in so well with our family. Cyrus and Annie love working with you in the kitchen and I can talk art with you. Mother thinks you are a genius and Lester would be interviewing you about all the things you are so well accomplished in. Are you sure you won't give Cyrus a little encouragement? We could stop back by here in a few weeks."

"Me, a genius?" Alice almost choked.

"Of course, but I was asking about Cyrus. He doesn't see many women that pique his interest. And to be honest not many women see him for the masculine man he is because he likes to cook. They think he's a bit of a sissy but you haven't treated him like that," Emma said.

"Cyrus a sissy?" Alice barely whispered. "Lord, he's so handsome Sadie stutters in front of him. And what's the matter with a man cooking? Not one thing. Women would have to be insane to think he's a sissy."

"Then you might at least think about him for the next month and not be adverse to us stopping back in Huttig for a couple of days?" Emma pushed on.

"I could probably do that," Alice agreed.

"Good. I'm going on in to get packed. We'll be leaving on the eight o'clock train heading south. It's been so much fun here, Alice. I really look forward to the return trip."

"And if you decide to stay in southern Louisiana, drop me a postcard so I won't be looking for you. And if there's a woman that Cyrus sees and is thunderstruck on the first sight, let me know that too," Alice said.

"I promise, but I've only seen Cyrus struck mute once in his life and that was at the train station when he saw you." Emma went back into the hotel.

The sun set in a glorious array of orange, brilliant pink and yellow through the trees that evening as Alice still sat on the porch. She heard the muted drone of voices in the lobby as one by one the family brought their luggage down for Ira to transport back to the train station. First he took the three men who waved at her as they departed. She was glad Cyrus hadn't made an effort to tell her good-bye privately. Hopefully his sister was seeing things that she wanted to see, even if they weren't really there. But then if he did have an attraction for Alice and the next month went the way she figured it would, she might be over Ira by then and there was a possibility she could fall for someone else.

Yes, there is a possibility. Like there is a possibility the devil will sprout big white wings and a halo. It ain't happening girl. You are in love with Ira and it'll take more than a month to get over him. You didn't even look at Cyrus when he left, you were so busy staring at Ira.

In a few minutes Ira returned to load the luggage into the Ford. When he drove away that time the ladies joined Alice on the porch. They each claimed a rocking chair and began to talk at once.

Annie was dressed in a lovely green suit with matching skirt and jacket, an ivory shirt, and she carried one of those new black morie clutch purses covered with tambour-style embroidered yellow flowers with green leaves.

"I'm sorry. You can't understand any of us when we chatter all at once but we've all got so many things to thank you for. This has been a wonderful two days and we'll always remember it. Emma has already suggested we stop by again if Mother decides to go back to New York," Annie said.

"Which I won't. They don't believe me but I've had enough cold winters to last me the rest of my life. However, we might just ride the train up here in a few weeks for a lark. If you'll let me in the kitchen again, it's a promise," Marlee said. She wore the same traveling suit she'd arrived in two days earlier but she looked more relaxed.

"And I want to thank you for the use of your art supplies. I'm not looking forward to another train ride but at least I won't be jumping out the window from pure boredom now that I've had a little reprieve," Emma said.

Her light brown suit was trimmed in ecru lace and Alice recognized the scent she wore as Muscade from Jerome. It had been her mother's favorite scent and she'd only worn it on special occasions.

"You are all so very welcome. Bridget and I've enjoyed the time with you as much as you have with us, I'm sure. We'll be looking forward to seeing you again, whether it's on the way back to New York or just for a visit. Put a postcard in the mail when you get there so we'll know you have made it safely," Alice said.

"We'll do one better. One of us will call you on the telephone." Emma winked.

"You ladies ready?" Ira called from the car.

"No, but we must go. I have to see it all the way to the coast before I make up my mind where I'm going to settle," Marlee said. "If you change your mind about selling the Swan, let me have first chance?"

"I will, but I won't," Alice said.

"You are a smart girl. You know what you've got and you'll hang on to it like a bulldog with a bone," Marlee said.

Alice just smiled. Two different people had called her smart. Of course neither of them were from Huttig. Maybe Alice needed to get out of Huttig and into an environment where no one knew that she'd been tagged "touched."

Dust kicked up behind the car as Ira drove away for the third time. She drew her knees up under her chin and wrapped her arms around them as she watched the dust settle back to the ground. It took about as long for it to drift back down to the ground as it did for her to dismiss the idea of ever leaving Huttig. Despite what people said or thought, it was home.

She heard Ella fussing and Bridget crooning but still she didn't go inside. It wouldn't be long until the wet season set in and sitting out on the porch in the evening wouldn't be an option. She needed to go strip the beds in six rooms, put fresh sheets on, dust — a thousand things to make the rooms ready for the next customers. But that could wait until the morrow. Right then Alice was bathing in the idea that someone else thought she was intelligent.

Ira returned and went straight back into the hotel without even stopping to say good night or ride the next poker to hell or anything in between. He did take time to speak to Bridget and Alice heard the word *Ella* more than once. Jealousy turned her heart to stone and her smile faded. The evening lost its glow and she stormed into the house and up the stairs.

She'd stripped the sheets off the bed in the room where Cyrus slept and was in the process of tossing them in the hall when Ira's door opened. He took one look at the expression on her face and folded his arms across his chest.

"So do they still smell like his shaving lotion? Do you miss him already?"

"What in the hell are you talking about?"

"Every sentence he spoke on the way to the station started with your name. I just figured maybe you two had hit it off pretty good," Ira said.

"I don't have to explain anything to you.

211

Remember, I'm witless," she reminded him.

"Those were your words, not mine. Did you kiss Cyrus too just to see if he might be the one?"

"That's none of your business, Ira Mc-Newel. And I wasn't smelling his dirty sheets. I was bringing them out here to pile up for the laundry lady to pick up tomorrow. Which is none of your business, either."

"You could do worse. He's rich. He's obviously smitten with you and he thinks you are the smartest thing since woman was created."

"I imagine I could do worse but you don't have to worry about it, do you? You'll be gone at Christmas and I'll never see you again so it's not your concern." She dropped the sheets and went into Emma's room that still smelled like Muscade. She shut her eyes and could visualize her mother in her Sunday best and smelling like that.

The vision stared at Alice with a frown instead of a smile like she usually had on Sunday. "Why do you vex that man when you love him? You are never going to catch him with vinegar. If you want him you've got to apply a little honey." Her mother's words came through as clearly as if she'd been standing in front of her.

"Need some help?" Ira asked.

"No I can do it myself."

"Then I'll wait until you get them in the hall and I'll tie them up in a bundle and put them by the front door for the laundry lady to pick up in the morning. Or should I drive them down and leave them on her porch so she can get an early start?"

"I said I don't want help. You could aggravate Jesus himself."

"And you couldn't?"

"Not as much as you. Here, if you're going to help then take these sheets out to the hall and strip off the bed in Robert's room."

"Yes, ma'am," he said smartly and went across the hall.

Working out their frustrations together, they had all six rooms cleaned and ready for the next round in an hour. Ira tied the sheets, towels, and washcloths together in bundles and pitched them down the stairs. "I'm taking these to the laundry tonight. Then I'm coming home and locking myself in my room and rereading those Zane Grey books I found in the basement."

"You didn't ask if you could read my books and those are for kids, not adults."

"Boy kids, not girl kids."

She bowed up to him. "I liked them so Daddy bought them when he went into El Dorado on business trips."

"And I like them now. They take my mind off . . ." He stopped.

"Off what?" she antagonized him.

"The war," he lied. It had been on the tip of his tongue to tell her that they took his mind off her. Granted they were written for young boys but at least they entertained him in the evenings.

"Good," she said and stomped down the stairs, wishing that her shoes made more noise than they did on the hardwood. She wasn't about to feel sorry for him because he'd had a bad experience in the war. So what if he'd been left for dead then resurrected? So what if he'd come home to find his family all gone and his fiancée married to someone else? It couldn't be a bit more painful or frustrating than living in the same house with him for five months, having December staring her in the face and being able to do nothing about it. Or wanting what she could never have. So let him read Zane Grey. At least it erased all his bad memories. She had nothing to erase the good ones like the kisses they'd shared or the conversations they'd had while they worked together.

Sadie arrived the next morning right on time and found Alice already in the kitchen, her hands deep in a bowl of ground beef, making meat loaf for dinner. "Got a little ahead of the schedule, didn't you? What's for breakfast?"

"Hotcakes with sausage. It's just us and Ira so it won't take long. I couldn't sleep," Alice said.

"Me neither. I got to thinking about that Cyrus and my eyes popped right open. I still can't imagine a man in the kitchen. But I'm here to tell you if his brother, Lester, would have offered to take me with him, I'd be gone today. That was the prettiest man I've ever laid my eyes on. Made me go stone crazy. Couldn't think of a word to say to him."

Ira joined them and poured himself a cup of coffee. "Need anything from the store? I'm going to town right after we eat to get some paint for the floor down in the basement."

"Potatoes," Alice said.

"Hundred pounds?"

"That would be good."

He carried his coffee to the dining room and found a chair. She was still mad and he had no idea what he'd done. He'd helped get the rooms in order, taken the laundry to town before he went to bed, where he'd stared at the ceiling for hours and hours.

Even if they ever did make some kind of a commitment, which they never would, he couldn't live with a woman like Alice. He'd either be crazy in the sight of a month or in jail for strangling her to death. If Bridget was as aggravating as Alice, he could almost understand Ralph's temper.

"No, I can't. A man doesn't hit a woman. Especially if he loves her," he muttered.

Bridget carried Ella into the room and drew up a chair beside him. "Good morning."

Ira sipped his coffee. "It is."

"Ella slept through the night except for two feedings. She's really a good baby, aren't you sweetheart."

"I like that picture Emma painted of you two. You should hang it above the mantel," Ira said.

"I've been thinking about doing that. I'll have to have it framed. What do you think? Oak or cherry?"

"Cherry. It'll bring out the color of your hair," he said.

"It would, wouldn't it?"

Sadie brought out a stack of pancakes and set them in the middle of the table. Alice followed with a plate of sausage patties and the syrup pitcher. Sadie went back for butter and a pitcher of milk. Bridget said grace

216

and they began to help plates.

Sadie was unusually pretty that day in her sprig green dress. Her hair had been braided and wrapped around her head in a crown. Ira tried to picture her hair down and his hands tangled up in it. She'd make a fine wife. She knew how to cook, clean, and loved her sister's children. She'd made eyes at him the whole six weeks he'd been back in Huttig and left no doubt that she'd be more than willing for a courtship.

Bridget was getting smaller every single day. She took great pains with her dress and strawberry blond hair and had the sweetest disposition of any woman Ira had ever known. He could start off with a ready-made family and add to it.

Alice had bags under her green eyes. Her hair had been twisted up the back of her head and several strands were sneaking out of the pins. She wore an old pair of striped overalls and a white shirt badly in need of ironing. She was barefoot and she was stubborn and opinionated. Not one thing to draw him to her and yet she was the one he kept stealing glances at while they ate breakfast.

He wiped his mouth on a napkin, stood up, and pushed his chair back under the table. "Thank you for a good meal. I'll be going to the store now. Think of anything else you need?"

"Salt," Sadie said.

"Potatoes and salt, then."

"And could you pick up some white thread for me?" Bridget asked.

"Three things, plus the paint," he said.

"Sign the bill for it. Tell Minnie I'll settle it when I come in for supplies on Monday," Alice said.

Ira nodded and headed out the door.

"I could help with the cakes today," Bridget said.

"You can sit on a chair and watch us. You aren't lifting anything heavier than Miss Ella for a while longer. I know you are getting stir crazy, but listen to the doctor," Alice said.

"I'm sick of our bedroom and the living room back there. I'm tired of bed rest and I'm not doing it anymore. Bring me a chair to the kitchen. I can peel potatoes sitting," she said.

"Oh, okay, but that's all. And what do you intend to do with Ella while you are peeling potatoes?" Sadie asked.

"Alice is going to pull her cradle in here. I grew up in the kitchen. Ella can do the same," Bridget said.

"You planned this?" Sadie asked.

218

"For two days. I'd have been here sooner if I hadn't sat for that picture business."

Thirty minutes later Ira carried a hundred pounds of potatoes into the kitchen on his shoulder. In his other hand he held a box of salt and a spool of white thread, which he set on the counter. "Alice, could I have a word with you?"

She'd been making chocolate icing for the cakes and had a smudge on her cheek. Her apron was testimony that she'd made meat loaf while he was gone and the kitchen smelled like rising yeast rolls. He straightened his back and took one more look at her in her element. He wished he could have seen her just once more all intense as she worked on a painting.

She followed him out of the kitchen expecting to discuss the floor in the basement and hoping that he didn't say anything about the way she'd been acting. She had no words to explain her actions, at least not without baring her heart and soul.

"I didn't tell you but I wrote to my grandparents last week. I told them I was alive and working for you here at the Black Swan and that I'd be out to see them right after Christmas," he blurted out.

"That's wise. At their age a shock like seeing you standing in their doorway wouldn't be good for them," she said.

"I got a letter this morning. My grandfather has died and my grandmother needs me. She wants to move in with my aunt in Greenville but there's the farm to consider. Cotton is almost ready to be picked and the tobacco is hanging in the sheds ready to be graded. She has a few men working for her but she's old and she's tired. She wants me to come to Mississippi and run the farm. I'm the last McNewel so Grandpa had made a will and left the farm to Grandma, but when she goes it's to be given to me. She said in her letter that she doesn't want me to wait until she's dead. She's deeding it over to me as soon as I get there. I didn't know any of this but I've got to go help her. I hope you won't be too upset with me for running out on you like this."

I can't breath. I want to cry. I can't endure watching you leave. I love you. My heart is breaking in half.

"Of course I'm not upset with you. You've got a farm to run, tobacco to grade, and cotton to pick. I wouldn't be much of a friend if I made you stand by your word when there's all that to do. So I give you back your word to work until Christmas. When are you leaving? I'll need to pay you for this past week before you go." She was utterly amazed that words came out of her mouth without sobs and pleading.

"Thank you. I bought a ticket on the noon train going toward Greenville. From there I'll catch the one to Grace and I should be there by bedtime."

"Today?"

So fast? Lord, how will I bear it?

He nodded.

"Then you'd better be getting your things together. I'll get your pay for the week out of the cash register," she said.

"Alice, I want to thank you for the job. For letting me live here. Everything that you've done."

"You are very welcome. And you earned every dime and more of what I'm paying you, Ira. I never thought of you on a farm. I just figured someday the mill would be running overtime again and you'd be back here sometime," she said.

"I love farming. I was just a little kid when Dad decided to move here. He didn't like the cotton and tobacco crops. Hated depending on the weather for his living. Said he'd rather work anywhere but the farm," Ira said.

She didn't want him to go. Not just yet. Keeping him beside her just another minute was as important as taking her next breath.

"How big is it, the farm?"

"A section. Six hundred and forty acres. The house isn't much. Grandpa let it get run-down these past few years. Not much more than a sawmill home, actually. We lived in one similar only smaller about a quarter of a mile down the road. I expect it's still standing too. Grandma's house has two bedrooms and a big old living room–kitchen combination. She did what she could to make it nice," he reminisced. Just a little more time with Alice. He'd never see her again and his heart ached at the idea, but there wasn't a thing he could do about it.

"You'll do fine," she said.

"Well, I guess that's it then. I might have time to paint the floor before I leave," he said.

"No, you just get your things ready and I'll drive you to the station about eleven thirty. And Ira, take those Zane Grey books with you."

"Thank you."

Her heart and soul did a nosedive and fell at her feet.

She couldn't have put food in her mouth at noon but she did pack a sack full of meat loaf sandwiches and chunks of chocolate cake for Ira to take on the train with him. Knowing him he'd be sharing with any hungry soldier so she'd made sure there was plenty. She drove him to the station and sat beside him on the bench on the side where the train would come to a stop.

"So what will you do with the rest of your life?" he asked out of the clear blue.

"What I do every day. Cook. Clean. Take care of Bridget and Ella. Look forward to Catherine's visits."

"Think you'll marry someday?"

"Probably," she said, but she didn't convince herself.

"He'll be a lucky guy."

She didn't answer.

"Here she comes," he said when the ground shivered beneath their feet moments before they could actually hear the train.

"I hope you really do like farming and that you have a wonderful life in Grace, Mississippi."

"Thank you, Alice. That means a lot. If I'm ever through this area again, I'll stop by. And if you are ever in Grace, come see me."

"I'll do that."

They were just words though. Something to fill the aching space because he'd never have cause to come back to Huttig. And she'd sure enough never have cause to travel to a little town called Grace.

They said good-bye without hugs or steamy kisses. He waved one last time when he boarded the train. She watched until there was no more noise or even a rumble under her feet.

When she got home to the hotel she built a roaring blaze in the fireplace. Bridget and Ella slept while she tore out pages and pages of drawings and burned them. Tears dripped from her cheekbones and soaked the front of her overalls but she kept tearing and burning until they were all gone.

She sat in front of the fire hugging an empty sketchbook and crying silently. Destroying eight years worth of drawings didn't erase a single vision of him. Every time she blinked she could see him.

CHAPTER FIFTEEN

Ira leaned the chair back until it sat on two legs. The night air had a bit of nip in it but not nearly enough to keep him inside. Will appeared from the side of the house and sat on the porch steps. Tall and lanky, the older man had skin the color of rich coffee with only a little bit of cream and eyes as black as midnight. His face was as wrinkled as a shirt fresh off the clothesline, before an iron had had time to do its job. His smile was spontaneous with big white even teeth but that night seriousness covered Will like a coat during a snow storm.

"You been readin' the papers?" he asked.

Ira nodded. "Mess, ain't it?"

Will had been on the McNewel farm since long before Ira was born. Back when his grandparents took over the operation from his great-grandfather, they'd hired Will to help out one summer and he just stayed on. He'd married but his wife was now dead,

225

his five children scattered across Mississippi and Arkansas, all educated and holding down responsible jobs. These days he lived in the house where Ira's father and mother lived before they moved to Huttig. Once a year his kids came home and stayed a few days with him. Other than that Will served as the foreman of the farm. When Ira arrived the month before he'd been surprised to learn that his grandmother had her bags and belongings all packed and was ready to move the next week.

"But, Grandma, I know nothing about this operation," he had said.

"You'll learn faster if I'm not here. Will can teach you. He knows more than me or your grandpa, either one. He's the one who's kept this place making a profit. Listen to him and you'll do well. Never borrow money from the bank. There's going to come a time when folks who owe will lose what they've got. Keep your fist close to your chest and be careful where you keep your profits. Will knows enough to guide you. I'm leaving you in good hands," she'd said.

Will sighed as if reliving some of his own memories.

"You all right?" Ira asked.

"I'm seventy-five years old, son. I was

born up near Jackson in '44 before they freed the slaves. My Momma worked in the big house and Daddy was a blacksmith for the plantation. You know all this though. I've seen us colored folks come a long way since the war. And now this business up in Elaine just reminds me how far we got to go yet."

"Change takes a long time, Will," Ira said.

"Over a hundred was massacred just because they asked for equal rights on their cotton crops."

"It was bound to happen after that shoot-out that wounded the sheriff. It don't make none of it right but all the white people would rally around and scream to the heavens about the colored folks being Bolsheviks after that. I'm glad none of your kids live in that area," Ira said.

"What can them soldiers be thinkin'? Just shootin' down the people because of their skin color. This thing is settin' us back. Seems like we take one step forward and then get pushed two steps back. The white power structure in Phillips County has formed a committee of seven men made of influential planters, businessmen, and elected officials to investigate the cause and you can bet your white hind end that it will be put on the heads of the black men. Won't no committee made up of that kind say that those black men were in that church talking about the price of cotton. They'll be saying they were in there on some communist business. Governor Brough said he was going to Elaine to get the right information; went back to Little Rock the next day and told the newspaper folks that the situation at Elaine was well handled and under control. That there was no danger of any lynching. It didn't happen that way though, did it? More'n a hundred dead and almost three hundred put in jail to be questioned. What's happening to those men's families?" Will said.

Ira shook his head. "It's hard to believe something like this can happen right here so close to us. I read in one paper that they called it an insurrection of the Negroes against the whites directed by the Progressive Farmers and Household Union of America. They're saying the whole thing was made for the purpose of banding colored folks together for the killing of white people."

"We both know better than that, don't we? That business was started to get the colored sharecroppers the same price for their cotton as the white people got for theirs. It's a sorry thing going on. Seventy-five years old and about to finish up my days and something like this to set my people back. Almost makes me wish I'd gone out with the flu like your folks did."

"Don't be talking like that, Will. I couldn't run this place without you. You got to stick around awhile longer to show me what to do. I'd have made a mess of the tobacco crop if you hadn't been here. And the cotton? How would I know which folks to let in to harvest for us and which ones will do more damage than good?" Ira said. "I'm sorry about this mess up there in Elaine and I'm real sorry that men are being treated like that because they are black instead of white. It's not right."

"Guess it ain't no different than the way some white folks treat others that haven't got as much money or ain't as smart," Will attempted to change the subject slightly.

That brought Alice to Ira's mind and suddenly his face went as serious as Will's.

"What's her name?" Will asked.

"Who?"

"Only two things can cause a man to look like you do. Politics and women. My problem tonight is politics. You've been a good listener and understood my plight on the woes of the colored race. So now it's my turn. Tell me who she is," Will said.

"Won't do a bit of good to talk about it."

"Never know. Didn't think it would do a bit of good to talk about that Elaine mess neither but it helped me to get it off my chest. Might do the same for you if you give it a chance. Besides, the work is finished for the day. Pickers has gone home. Tobacco is curing in the sheds without our help. What else we got to do but talk, son."

Despite skin color Ira felt as close to Will right then as he would have his own grandfather. If he shut his eyes he could envision Ezra McNewel saying the same things with the same inflection as Will. Both were educated. Ezra to the eighth grade back when that was enough education for a farmer. Will, after he came to work for Ezra when he was in his midthirties. He'd wanted to learn to read and write and Ezra had taught him. Sometimes Will's language left no doubt that he was a black man; other times he sounded and spoke like the educated man he was.

Will raised an eyebrow above his dark eyes. "Well?"

"I was engaged to Catherine O'Shea in Huttig back before I went to the war," Ira said. "In all those months I was laid up I figured out I was marrying her for all the wrong reasons. You see, her momma named the three girls for the elements. Catherine for earth; Alice for air; Bridget for water. And she knew exactly what she was doing because that's the way they turned out."

Will waited patiently for the next part of the story.

"Anyway, I asked Catherine to marry me because she was as solid and steady as dirt," Ira said.

"Pretty or ugly as a mud fence?"

"Oh, the O'Shea girls are all pretty. Catherine has this burgundy red hair and she's tall and slim. Good head on her shoulders. Make a wonderful wife and mother," Ira said.

"Just not your wife, huh?"

"That's right. I didn't love Catherine. I was just choosing the best possibility for a wife."

"So did you tell her that?"

"Didn't have to. When I got back to Huttig, she'd got word I was dead so she went on with her life and married another man. I saw her and it didn't even make me all sad or sorrowful. I was just glad she'd found someone that loved her like she deserves."

"Well, it ain't Catherine, so who is it?"

Ira didn't want to say her name because just thinking it hurt too badly.

"That water girl, Bridget?" Will asked.

"No, she married a man who beat on her and then disappeared. She divorced him and took back her own name then had his baby and named it Ella, after her mother, and O'Shea. So now everyone is going to call her a bastard since she doesn't have a father. Bridget said no father was better than the one she would've had with that sorry man. I don't think Bridget will ever marry again. She got broke from sucking eggs with that first man."

Will was intrigued and forgetting about the Elaine problem. "I'd say so. Where do you reckon he went?"

"Tell the truth, I smelled a rat on that story. I think those girls might've killed him and buried him somewhere or threw his rotten carcass in the river. But they ain't talkin' and I didn't figure it was none of my business so I didn't pressure the issue."

"So it's the middle one, Alice?"

Ira gulped and nodded.

"She a redhead too?"

"Not the same red as Catherine. She was a carrottop when she was young but it's mellowed out some. She's an artist. She can paint flowers that you'd swear you could smell they're so real, and landscapes that take your breath away."

"So why ain't you owned up to your feelings for her?" Will asked. "When me and Pearl was courtin' I didn't waste no time lettin' her know my feelings. If I had there would've been another man on her doorstep with a bouquet of wild flowers."

"I've known her since we were kids. We grew up together in Huttig. She's smarter than any woman I ever knew but she's let the whole town think she's touched." Ira tapped the side of his head with his forefinger. "Because of that she doesn't think she's as bright as Catherine or as pretty as Bridget and she wouldn't believe me if I did own up to my feelings. She'd just think I felt sorry for her and maybe even think I really did have feelings for her sister and was just marrying anyone."

"You'll never know if you don't speak up. You miss her?"

"All the time. We kissed twice and I keep remembering that, but we fought more than twice and I remember that too."

"Me and Pearl, Lord have mercy, but we could argue. I got to admit though, we could make up later and that was awful sweet. I miss her. Been fifteen years since she went on and I keep thinkin' every year she'll have a place ready for me and call me on. Guess it's takin' a while to get God talked into letting me into heaven."

Ira chuckled. He felt a little sorry for God if Alice got it in her head something was going to be done different. There wouldn't be angels enough to talk her out of it. One thing for sure, God and the angels better not take one thing for granted up there because it would all come to a screeching halt when Alice got there and began to reorganize the place.

"You thinkin' about Alice now, aren't you? I see it on your face."

"Guess I was. She can be a handful."

"And if she wasn't, you wouldn't be interested. Mealymouthed woman never was what a McNewel or a Gunnerson man would fall for. We like our women sassy. I guess I'll be getting on home now. You think on what I said. Don't let too much time go by or things might get plumb out of your control."

"I'll think on it," Ira said. "And I'm sorry for the way things are over in Elaine."

"Thing is this, Ira. I can't do one thing about that. I can feel sorry for it and worry it around in my mind because it ain't right. You can do something about your problem. Two of us men livin' out here on this farm. Me up there in my house and you in this one. All alone, the both of us. I'm too old and Pearl would haunt me for sure if I

234

looked at a woman to keep house for me. But you can do something about your house. Alice might like it out here on the delta. She could've liked them kisses as much as you did."

"Good night, Will. Guess we'll start the pickers at first light?"

"Guess we will. Maybe come Christmas I'll have you talked into going back over to Huttig and takin' care of your personal business?"

"We'll see," Ira said.

Will headed around the end of the house with a wave. "Guess we will."

He walked slower these days. Ira wondered if Ezra had walked like that before he died. If his grandfather had gotten old in the past six years since he'd been to Mississippi to see him, he'd been surprised to see that his grandma had indeed aged years and years since the last time he had been to Grace. Six years before she'd still been spry and everywhere at once. Nowadays, it took two tries for her to get out of the rocking chair and a meal that used to take an hour to put on the table now took two or more.

Ira didn't want to grow old alone but he didn't want to share his life and farm with someone he didn't love, either. Thinking about it all gave him a headache. He finally went into the house, drank a tall glass of chilled buttermilk, and washed up for bed. Daybreak came early on the delta and the pickers would be waiting at the end of the rows with their sacks ready for first light. His job was to oversee the whole operation. Thank goodness Will would be right there with him.

He crawled into bed and laced his hands behind his head. It was the bed his parents had used their whole married life. It, along with several other pieces of furniture, had found their way into the house when his grandmother had picked and chosen what she wanted to take with her. He was grateful for all of it because it made the house more like his home.

For a while there he'd actually entertained notions of going back to Huttig and telling Alice exactly how he felt. But that was just dreams in the sky. Even though he wasn't poor anymore and owned a working, productive farm, he still wasn't good enough for Alice. She could be a famous artist and she was used to the hustle and bustle of a hotel, not the loneliness of a farm with only him and Will. He might have a few dollars hidden away and two good crops coming out of the ground this year but Alice deserved more. If he kept his distance she'd find someone like one of those Rosenthal fellows who'd stayed at the Black Swan. The one who liked to cook seemed quite taken with her. Perhaps they'd come back by on their way home to New York City and she'd be open-minded about that man if Ira stayed in Mississippi.

He groaned at the thought of someone else kissing Alice. Of another man running his fingers through that mass of red hair or brushing a strand back out of her face. Life just wasn't damn fair.

Alice drew her knees up and wrapped her arms around them. The night breezes smelled of the recent rain, all clean with just the right nip of fall in the air. Winter would come along soon and with it the rainy season, maybe a little snow or ice, but mostly just wet and cold. Until it arrived she would sit on the porch every evening and enjoy being outside as much as possible.

The moon was a big old outhouse moon shape with a few stars paying homage around it. She wondered if Ira was in Grace, Mississippi, looking at the same moon. Maybe with another woman. That caused her to inhale deeply. No one else had the right to admire the moon with her Ira.

Bridget brought Ella out and claimed a rocking chair. "It's a lovely night but a bit chilly for a three-month-old baby so I'll only stay a minute."

"She's so pretty, Bridget. She reminds me more and more of Momma," Alice said.

"Named her right, didn't I? Well, she'll fuss if I have to cover her face and this air will give her the colic for sure so we're going back inside. Annie and Emma will give her lots of attention so maybe she won't whine too long because she has to go back in."

Bridget and Cyrus passed each other in the doorway. He sat down in the same rocking chair Bridget had vacated. "Lovely evening. By now it's snowing in New York most likely. The holiday parties will start this week with Thanksgiving and go on through New Year's. There'll be a short break and then another burst of merrymaking at Valentine's Day."

"You've missed it, haven't you?" Alice said.

"Oh yes. Even Mother has finally said that she couldn't live anywhere else. We've loved the vacation. It's been wonderful but it's time to go home now. We miss our friends, the theater, the heartbeat of the city. Do you ever think of something or somewhere other than Huttig, Arkansas, Alice?"

"It's home just like New York is home to you."

"I could live here, you know. I love the kitchen and I could invest in this hotel. Make it a getaway place for the city folks who want a quiet holiday. A little advertising. A little spicing of the menu. We could have quite the enterprising business."

"You could live here but your heart would always be in New York."

"My heart would learn to love it here if it had a reason to stay."

She didn't answer because she had no idea what to say. His voice was low and husky and it was appealing to know that he was flirting with her. She wondered what Ira would think, then got angry at herself for caring. He'd been gone two months without so much as a penny postcard to let her know he'd arrived safely in Grace. For all she knew he'd died with some mysterious infection on the way. His grandmother would have no way of knowing she should inform anyone in Huttig. After all, to her knowledge, the Black Swan was just a place where he worked.

"What are you thinking about right now this minute?" Cyrus asked.

"Grace."

"Who is Grace?"

"Not who. Where. It's just a town over in Mississippi. I always thought it would be nice to live in a town with a pretty name. Huttig sounds so harsh and German, don't you think? Grace, now that sounds like a soft, laid-back place where there's magnolia trees and azaleas. I have trouble painting magnolias and azaleas. They've always given me fits."

Cyrus smiled. She was an eccentric little dove and he couldn't put his finger on why he was even drawn to her. Normally he liked dark-haired women with full figures. Maybe it was because she knew he was rich enough to buy the whole state of Arkansas if he wanted it and having that much money didn't impress her one bit. Every other woman he'd ever known saw dollar signs long before they saw Cyrus Rosenthal for himself.

"Could you ever be happy somewhere else?" he asked.

"I'm sure I could. After all, a place is just a place. Home is where the heart is and I reckon if my heart was there I'd have to call it home. Why do you ask?"

"We're leaving in the morning before you even have time to make breakfast. We'll have it on the train. I could make my home right here in Huttig and go visiting in New York maybe for the holiday season each year. Six weeks in the winter to see my family and friends then come back. If I had a reason to stay I might think seriously about having breakfast right here tomorrow."

Alice understood exactly what he was saying but she chose not to answer him. How could she? The whole time he'd been sitting there her mind had been on Ira and whether or not he was enjoying the same weather as she was, whether he was looking at the moon. But then Ira had said his good-byes and they were most likely permanent if the past two months was any indication. Cyrus was right there offering to actually live in a remote little sawmill town if she wasn't willing to go with him to New York.

Alice in New York City? She almost giggled but checked in time. She wouldn't hurt his feelings for anything. He was serious and it might be her only chance to get out of Huttig and see the world, have a family, be a part of a big family that already loved her. Loved Alice and didn't care or even know about her reputation for being slightly off-kilter. It was surely something to think about, all right.

"I see I've struck you speechless. I didn't mean to stun you, Alice. It's just that I've not been able to get you off my mind. I'm going inside now and if you think there is a reason for me to have breakfast in this hotel instead of getting on that train tomorrow morning, just let me know. I'll be in my room all night. Good night — and I'm very serious."

"Good night, Cyrus, and thank you," she whispered.

After a while she heard the guests go upstairs to their rooms and Bridget take Ella back to their bedroom. It was near midnight when she finally left the rocking chair behind and headed toward the cemetery. If only the elder Ella was alive to advise her, the decision might be easier to make.

She stood in front of the tombstone. "Momma, there's this good man who's all but proposed to me tonight. He's not like the last one who was trying to get his hands on the hotel. This man is really, really rich and I think he cares about me, not what I've got or can do for him. He's even offered to stay in Huttig and help with the Black Swan. He's a chef and a very good one so he'd be an asset. I could live in New York City, Momma. There are art galleries there and I could maybe someday be a famous artist. Cyrus says that my paintings are very good and his sister knows all the right people."

She backed up and sat on the granite rock with her parents' names engraved on the front. "Poppa, he's quite a catch. He'd treat me right and his sisters love me and I like his mother. They'd never need to know that I have thin air filling my head instead of a real brain. They all think I'm smart. Now that's something, isn't it? You'd even like them. They're not all uppity and they roll up their sleeves and work in the kitchen when they stay at the Swan. Daddy, tell me what to do, please."

An owl hooted in the distance.

A lonely cricket sang a solo behind another tombstone.

Two frogs provided a duet in deep-throated unison.

No answers came from either of her parents.

Alice walked back home, her mind made up even without their help.

Ira McNewel was in the past.

She had to get on with her life and forget him.

CHAPTER SIXTEEN

It didn't seem like three months since Ira had boarded the train in Huttig for Grace. It felt more like thirty years. He paced the boardwalk in front of the train stop, picked up his worn suitcase a dozen times, and then set it back down impatiently. Finally the rumble under his feet told him the train was there and he couldn't get on it fast enough. Four hours and he'd be in Huttig.

Will had told him to think about it that night on the front porch and that's all he'd done since then — think about Alice. He wasn't going with expectations of Alice falling at his feet with declarations of love and passion. Just to see her and hopefully kiss her one time before he left. That would be enough for this trip.

He found a seat beside an elderly lady and sat down. She was almost as wide as she was tall and had no less than three chins that wobbled when she laughed. Her blue eyes were sapphires set in a jolly round face and her southern voice soft and sweet.

"So tell me, young man, are you one of those soldiers off looking for work?" she asked.

"I was last fall but now I'm a cotton and tobacco farmer," he said.

"Now how did you get into that business?"

"My grandfather left it to me."

"Good timing. I'm May Ruth Simpson on my way to Little Rock. Got a daughter up there I'm going to stay with a few months. I been down in this area with my son and it didn't work out. House ain't big enough for two women, especially if one is a daughter-in-law. Guess it sure don't work if the other one is a mother-in-law," she giggled. "If all goes well in Little Rock, I might sell my place up in Greenville. If it don't, I'll just go back home and live out the rest of my days there."

"Would you know Mavis McNewel? She just recently moved there from Grace to live with my aunt."

"Why of course I know Mavis. She lives four doors down the street. Sweet woman but she ain't one to take no guff off nobody. My daughter-in-law wouldn't have a chance with Mavis. She wouldn't have stayed a whole week like I did. First time that snippy woman made Mavis mad she would have walked right out the door. Me, I stayed the whole time, miserable as it was. So it's the McNewel farm down in Grace that you inherited?"

"That would be it," Ira said.

His frazzled nerves had begun to settle down with a little conversation. His heart had calmed to a steady beat. His hands weren't clammy anymore.

"So you going to Greenville to see Mavis?"

"Actually I'm on my way to Huttig, Arkansas, to see a friend," he said. Now wasn't that stretching the truth more than an inch? He didn't know if Alice was his friend or not. She might take one look at him and tell him where to go and which poker to ride to reach those fiery gates.

"Male or female? Don't look at me like that. I'm an old woman. I can be nosy if I want to. It's one of the benefits of not dying young. We can say what we want and ask personal questions and everyone just says, 'Don't mind her, she's old.' I love being seventy years old. I can eat what I want, say what I want, and to the devil with anyone who don't like it, so answer my question, Ira McNewel. Yes, I know your name. Knew it before I ever spoke to you. You are the spitting image of your grandfather, Ezra. They used to ride the train up to visit their daughter and I'd see them about once a year. So, male or female?"

Ira grinned in spite of his attempts to keep from it. "Female."

"Well, I hope she's more than just a friend. Man needs help to run a farm as big as the McNewel place. Needs a good meal on the table at night and clean sheets on the bed. You be nice to her. Maybe things will work out to where you'll have what you need."

"Yes, ma'am," he said.

"Now, I'm going to take a nap. You'll have to change trains in Greenville and catch the one going on west. Don't wake me to say good-bye. I'm hoping to sleep most of the way to Little Rock. I hate trains. They get us where we're going faster than anything else but it's unnatural to wake up in Mississippi and go to bed in the middle of Arkansas."

"Guess so," Ira said.

Mrs. Simpson was snoring loudly within five minutes and his nerves began to fray as the countryside sped past. Four hours and he'd be in Huttig. Such a short time to try to figure out exactly what he was going to say to Alice. At Greenville, he left his riding buddy asleep and had a thirty-minute wait before the next train going to Huttig and El Dorado. He felt cooped up inside the station, but the bitter north wind drove him from the bench outside. A family with four wild little boys entertained him for the half hour that stretched on to eternity. The oldest one was only about seven, and from what Ira overheard they were on their way to a wedding in Huttig and were barely going to make it on time. When the train came to a stop the boy's mother gathered them up and hurried them out to board.

As if rushing around will make the train get there any sooner. I wonder who is getting married? he thought as he meandered out to find himself a seat. Alice would tell him when he arrived. She knew everything about everyone. The only difference in her and Mabel was that Mabel was vicious and spread gossip. Alice simply knew and never said a word or judged anyone for their actions.

When the train came to a halt in Huttig the family with the little boys were the first ones off and almost running toward the Commercial Hotel. The whole front lawn was filled with automobiles of every description, horse and buggies and wagons. He wondered why on earth a wedding would be going on at the hotel instead of in a church as he passed on his way to the Black Swan.

"Hello," he yelled as he opened the front door. The lobby was decorated for the holiday with green boughs on the mantle above the fireplace that glowed with dying embers. The room was warm and empty-feeling and there were no aromas of fresh baked bread coming from the kitchen.

"Hello. Anybody home?" He raised his voice higher.

He checked the dining room and kitchen to find both empty. Then the clock chimed one time. There was no way everyone would have finished their lunch by one o'clock. Something had to be terribly wrong.

He was halfway across the lobby when Mabel rushed in the front door and went straight back to the Alice and Bridget's private quarters. She returned so quick he scarcely had time to blink and she carried a bridal veil and a bouquet of poinsettias wrapped with a wide white satin ribbon with her.

"Well, Ira McNewel, what are you doing in Huttig today?"

"I . . . ," he stammered.

"Well, you shouldn't be here. Get on the

train and go back to Mississippi. That's where you should be today. Not here. There's a wedding going on at the Commercial Hotel. You sure don't need to be there. I know the bride had a thing for you and God only knows she's getting a much better deal with the new feller she's marrying up with today. So go home."

"But . . ." He blushed.

"I've got to run. I can't stand here and explain this whole thing to you. Just go home. The Rosenthals are waiting. The bride forgot her veil and Bridget forgot her bouquet. She's the matron of honor, or is it the maid of honor since she's an O'Shea again? It's all very confusing. The wedding starts at one thirty. I've got to go. You get on the next train back to your farm."

"Please . . . ," he started.

She threw up her hand holding the poinsettias. "Go home. You shouldn't even be here."

He picked up his suitcase and headed back to the train station. He should have listened to Will and done something about his feelings for Alice sooner. He'd forsaken her and now she was marrying that Rosenthal man who liked to cook with her in the kitchen. She'd go off to New York City. Maybe that was the way things should be. After all, she was an artist and the big city would give her an outlet for her work. All he could offer her was a white frame house surrounded by acres of cotton and tobacco, an aching back at the end of the day, and all the love in his heart. Not much of a comparison when compared to a life in New York City with a rich man.

The next train to Greenville didn't leave for an hour so he sat down to wait again, this time with no little boys to run hither and fro. He'd been sitting there thirty minutes, off in his own world of woe and self-loathing for not doing one thing about what was in his heart, when he felt a presence beside him. Hoping he was wrong and knowing he wasn't, hoping it would be Alice and yet realizing she wouldn't be coming to the train station immediately after her wedding, he turned to find Major sitting beside him. The man had been old when Ira was a little boy and hadn't changed much since then. He'd lost his family to the flu the previous year and only worked at the mill a couple of days a week, leaving him time to fish and visit.

"Saw you sittin' here through the window over there and thought I'd come on in and visit a spell," Major said.

"Too cold to fish?" Ira asked.

251

"Freeze my ears off if I tried to fish right now. Besides, the fish is layin' up at the bottom of the river gettin' fat for the springtime. They ain't interested in no old man with a hook and line this time of year," Major said.

"North wind is a bit cold, ain't it?" Ira said.

"Can't imagine a wedding on a day like this. There's one going on in the Commercial Hotel today. Groom is one of them Jew people so he didn't want to have the wedding in a Christian-type church building, so the little bride, bein' the sweetheart she is, said they could have it in the Commercial. Place looked packed when I come by there. They've got a big reception going after. She invited me but Lord Almighty, that many people a millin' around would give me a case of hives. I did sneak in and take a look at the bride. Pretty as a picture in that white lace dress, and you should see the cake, Ira. It's five tiers high with red flowers on the top. Got sugar icing. I told her if there's a piece left to give it to the night clerk to hide under the counter for me. I heard tell they're going over the water for their honeymoon. Somewhere over there in France or Italy. Guess when you've got that kind of money, you can spend it that way. Seems to me like a big change for a little old girl who's used to cooking at the Black Swan."

"They say love will make you do crazy things," Ira said.

"Well, boy, tell me what are you doin' back here? Surely you didn't come for the weddin' and then not go. Can't really see the bride invitin' you since she was sweet on you for a while. Might be a little strange to know you're a settin' there when she's sayin' her vows and all."

"Actually, I just came . . . Oh, it doesn't matter. There's my train, Major. You stay warm. Looks like we're in for a cold winter." Ira picked up his suitcase.

"I reckon you came on account of Miss Alice. Don't look so surprised, Ira. I knew you was sweet on her when you were there. Lord, boy, the way you looked at her reminded me of the way I looked at my wife back when we was young. Never did understand why you asked Catherine to marry you when it was Alice that made you go all soft in the eyes."

"Well, it's too late for that now, isn't it?" Ira said and hurried out to the train before Major got started on something else to tear the rest of his mangled heart into shreds.

Once the train left the tall pines behind

everything was as barren as Ira's soul. What few trees sped past the train window was just naked limbs reaching out to a gray sky devoid of color. The ground was brown with dead grass. Even the barbed-wire fences looked cold and uninviting.

Ira stared out at a future as bleak as the scenery. A long, long life of just him and Will on the farm, and then just him. No one to leave the land to since he couldn't envision anyone other than Alice sharing his life. When the train pulled into the station, he picked up his suitcase again and began the long walk home. Five miles of cold wind that was warm compared to the ice in the middle of his chest.

A mile down the road he dropped the suitcase and sat down on it. Dark was settling in and Ira had let himself wallow around in the pity pool long enough. He gave himself a severe lecture aloud concerning his own negligence and with renewed spirit he walked on for another mile.

Yellow light shined out from the windows of his nearest neighbor. The house was much bigger than the one he occupied, but then it needed to be larger. The man and woman who lived on that two-section farm had two sons and two daughters. The sons had gone to war and come home in one piece. Most families would consider getting one son home alive a miracle; to have two come back was sheer magic. The oldest daughter would be about twenty-three and the next one twenty-one. They'd come around to make themselves known with an apple pie back in the fall. The older daughter had light brown hair she wore in a tight little bun on the top of her head. Just looking at her let Ira know she was a no-nonsense woman who'd run a farm with a fist of iron and raise up children the same way. If he wanted a McNewel son to leave in charge of his land, that might be the woman to bear it for him.

He pondered on that for mile three but changed his mind by the time he started the fourth mile. If he couldn't marry for love then he'd be an old bachelor who raised cotton and socked the money away to give to his cousins. No nieces and nephews for Ira; the flu took care of that. But his father's sister, the woman his grandmother had gone to live with, had four daughters. All married, they had lots of children who could stand to inherit a tidy little sum in the future.

In the middle of the fourth mile it began to drizzle, forming ice as it stuck to the tree limbs and barbed-wire fences. Ira was glad he was nearly home and that he'd worn both a scarf and knitted cap when he reached up and the hair hanging down on his forehead was frozen solid.

His house was dark and he didn't bother to light a lamp when he went inside. He found his way to his bedroom, shucked out of his cold wet clothes, and slipped beneath the sheets, covered up with three heavy quilts and warmed up a spot. He was glad the day was over and he was back in his own surroundings. He'd never go to Huttig again. The memories of how hard that wedding hit him would fade eventually, but every time he thought of the place it would bring pain. He couldn't imagine standing in the Black Swan or walking past the Commercial Hotel and not hurting all over again.

At dawn he finally drifted off into sleep troubled with dreams of Alice: the day she fell off the ladder and knocked him flat on his back. The feel of her body next to his even when he was half starved. The way she had hugged him after she told him about his family all dying from the flu and cared enough to feed him before she gave him the news. The day they rode home from the cemetery on the bicycle, only to crash in the front yard. The way her lips felt on his that day in the basement. Her red hair constantly escaping from the braids she wrapped around her head. All of it replayed over and over in his restless dreams.

The rain had stopped when he awoke. He glanced out the window and ice sparkled like diamonds on the trees. The warmth of the sun had already begun to melt it but the sight was beautiful. He pulled a shirt on over his long handles and was hitching up his overalls when he smelled bacon frying. Will had never come into the house and cooked breakfast. They always met on the front porch in the mornings. Ira had a cup of coffee and Will carried a mason jar full of sweet tea.

He raised his nose and sniffed again. It was bacon for sure. Why would Will leave his own house and cook in Ira's? Especially when Will thought he was in Huttig. Ira shoved his feet into socks and plodded out across the living room and through the door to the kitchen.

"It's about time you got up. Sun's been up for an hour. I heard you come in last night but I figured you were plumb tuckered out so I didn't bother you. You want three eggs or four this morning?" Alice asked.

"You are married and going to France and you are wearing eyeglasses," he said.

"Where'd you get a fool notion like me

257

getting married and going to France? And yes, I'm wearing eyeglasses. I ordered them from Sears and Roebuck and I can see so well I'm constantly mad at myself for waiting so long to order them. And three eggs or four? Tell me before the grease gets cold and they end up with hard yolks. I know how you hate that."

"Your eyes look huge and even greener with the glasses. I went to Huttig," he whispered, unable to grasp the fact that Alice was in his kitchen.

"I know. That sweet man, Will, who lives in the house just over there told me you'd gone to Huttig. He said I could just come in and make myself at home. Will you please tell me how many eggs you want?"

He picked a number, not sure if he could swallow a single bite. "Four."

She cracked two into the hot bacon grease. "Will said you went to Huttig. Isn't that funny? You went there on the same day I came here."

He was still stunned. "But Mabel said you were getting married and I couldn't go to the wedding and for me to come back home."

"Are you sure she said I was getting married? I think you misunderstood her. It was Sadie getting married. Lester Rosenthal took a shine to her when they came back through on their way to New York. They've been writing and he came to see her a couple of times before he proposed and she accepted." She deftly slipped the eggs onto a turner and out to his plate and cracked two more into the grease. "She asked me to stand up with her but I couldn't. Not when Cyrus was going to be standing up with Lester. That would be just too too weird after he'd wanted me to say I'd marry him. I thought I might but I just couldn't say the words to him. He's a good man, Ira, but anyway, here's your breakfast. Sit up here and eat. I bet you didn't have supper did you?"

He was more than glad to sit. His legs didn't feel like they would support him another minute. He'd no sooner plopped down into the kitchen chair than the anger set in. What was she doing here? Ladies didn't go visiting men. They waited for the men folks to come visit them. Why hadn't she stayed home and waited?

She put his plate in front of him and went back to the stove to fry an egg for her breakfast. "You've got a nice house here, Ira. It's a bit strange with so few trees but I bet the sunsets are gorgeous. Aren't you going to say a thing, Ira? You said if I was ever in the area to come see you and I did and you aren't saying anything. You'd better eat that before it gets cold. They'll be greasy if you don't."

"Don't be coming in here telling me how to eat my breakfast. If I want to wait until noon to eat it, it's my business."

"You sure are cranky. I don't remember you acting like this in the morning. Usually you were happy at breakfast. Oh, was it Sadie? Good Lord! That's why you are angry, isn't it? It took three months for me to convince myself to come here and it was Sadie you liked. She did like you but Ira, she loves Lester. God, I'm sorry to have to be the one to tell you bad news every time."

Alice could have thrown herself on the floor and pitched a howling fit. For three months she'd moped about, almost convinced herself to marry a man she didn't love, and now she'd come to Grace to find that Ira had been in love with Sadie. Those two kisses they'd shared hadn't meant a thing to him. They hadn't curled his toenails and made his heart race the way they had hers.

"I'll get my things together and walk on back to town. I was lucky yesterday. Your neighbor lady down the road a couple of miles saw me headed this way and gave me a ride. The sun will melt the ice soon and it'll warm up. I'm sorry Sadie wasn't there for you, Ira. You deserve at least one lucky break in your life." The words poured out and she was able to keep the tears at bay until she shut the bedroom door where she'd slept the night before.

Ira sat there in dumbfounded silence, his food growing colder by the minute. She stayed in the bedroom for a few minutes and carried a small suitcase with her when she returned. Without a word she marched to the front door and walked out of his life. She'd cleared the yard and had the gate open when he rushed to the door and called out to her.

"Alice, don't go. Come back in here. You'll freeze to death."

She didn't even look back. She couldn't. For three long agonizing months she'd missed him, wanted to feel his arms around her, and he'd been nothing but rude since he awoke that morning. She'd done nothing wrong but love a man who loved another woman. But then, what could she expect? Ira McNewel was a land owner now, not a poor man without even a few cents to buy his dinner. He wouldn't be interested in Alice for a friend, much less fall in love with her.

Bridget had told her she was dashing off on a fool's errand and she'd be back in Huttig by the end of the week. She'd been right again only she'd be back in Huttig in barely more than twenty-four hours.

"Alice, I said come back. We need to talk," he said.

She kept walking. Why did they need to talk? So that she could hear him say the words that would be like scalding hot bacon grease to her heart? That he could never love her and that she had no right to come to his home without an invitation?

Ira ran out of the house without stopping to put on his shoes, dashed across the crunchy ice-covered grass, and through the gate. "Alice, please stop and let me explain."

She turned around and glared at him when he touched her arm. "There's nothing to talk about or explain. I was a complete fool but that's not so unusual, is it? I guess they were right about me all the time. I've got nothing but air between my ears. If I had a brain I'd have known you could never —"

He shoved both hands deep in his pockets to keep from throwing them around her and begging her to stay. "Please come back inside the house. My feet are freezing out here and I want you to stay. I'm sorry I

262

acted like that."

"Really?" She cocked her head off to one side. Men! They were the strangest of creatures. What was it about them that attracted sensible women to them anyway?

"Please."

"All right but only for one hour. That's how long you've got to explain to me why you got all huffy when all I did was make your breakfast and let you sleep."

"Deal," he said and then made a running dash for the door.

By the time she got back he had his socks off and his scarlet red feet propped close to the fireplace trying to warm them. She set the suitcase inside the doorway and removed her coat and hat. It was his turn to talk so she sat on the settee and waited. The room was a bit too fussy for her taste with all the glass birds and animals strewed about on every small table, each one covered with a doily and crammed into every inch of space. The red-and-white checkered curtains clashed with the pink roses in the wallpaper, which fought with the dark blue floral settee. It was so busy it came nigh onto giving her a headache, but it was Ira's house, not hers.

"You going to say anything?" he asked after a few minutes of pressured silence.

"You didn't eat your food."

"That's all?"

"I'd say it's your turn, not mine."

"This ain't the Black Swan Hotel."

"I noticed."

"You making fun of my house?"

"I just noticed it wasn't a hotel is all."

"Would you take a ride with me before you go running off? I'll get the truck out of the barn if you'll go with me."

"I guess I could take time for that. I've come all this way. I don't suppose an hour more would kill me."

"I've got to get more socks and my shoes and coat. You'll stay right here until I get them?"

"I said I'd go for the ride with you, Ira. I won't run away while you get yourself wrapped up to go."

"I want you to see my land, Alice. I never dreamed Grandpa would leave this place to me. Never thought I'd be the last of the McNewel males to be alive. I was the one who went to war and came out of it alive. The rest stayed home and are gone. It's a lot to think about."

"Well, praise the Lord, you can talk without biting my head off."

He headed toward his bedroom for dry socks and shoes. "I'm trying to explain something to you and you are snapping at me now."

"Fairly so, I might say. I'm glad you have all this Ira and I believe you will do well with it. I'll take a ride with you on one condition. That when we are done you'll drive me to the train station. It's too dang cold out there to walk five miles and tote a suitcase at the same time."

"When we are finished, if you want to go to the train station, I promise to take you there," he agreed.

CHAPTER SEVENTEEN

The truck was so old it had rust spots on it but it still ran as smoothly as if it had just come off the assembly line. Ira opened the door for Alice, got her settled into the wide front seat, and wrapped a heavy patchwork quilt around her legs. If he would have simply laid his hands on her thighs she wouldn't have needed the warmth of the cover, but she didn't tell him that.

She didn't care what he was taking her to see. Nothing could erase the agitated feeling of stupidity churning around in her chest. Bridget had tried to talk her out of this trip but she'd been hell-bent on seeing Ira again. Just one more time to make absolutely sure he didn't love her the way she did him. Bridget had been right again. Alice must remember to listen to her younger sister more often. So what if she was unstable as a glass of water; she knew men better than Alice did.

"Okay, the property starts at the road out there. The house sits in the southeast corner of the farm. A quarter of a mile down this road is where I was born and grew up. Will lives in that house now. It's right there." He stopped the truck and waved at Will, who carried a jar of tea with him as he left the porch and started down to the main house. "It's got two bedrooms and a big living room, kitchen, and dining room all in one. The outhouse is down the path to the left there. I guess you found the one at my house?"

She nodded. Good Lord, had he brought her out here to discuss outdoor bathrooms?

"Okay, we'll go on. The tobacco operation is a hundred and fifty acres back behind Will's house. We had a good year according to Will. It's been harvested and the money is safe. This is the section line." He made a hard left-hand turn and the truck bounced along frozen tracks with nothing but pot-holes and dead grass instead of a proper road.

"My property goes a mile back down this way. You can see the tobacco land right there on your left. We'll plow the stalks back in the ground come spring for natural fertilizer. Thank goodness for Will and his knowledge. I hope he doesn't die for a long time because I feel so inadequate to take over all this. I expected my grandmother to help me learn the ropes when I got here but she left the next week, saying that Will would teach me. But he's seventy-five years old. Spry as a young chicken but there's few guarantees at that age."

Maybe he'd brought her on this little ride to show her his place, much like she'd shown him the Black Swan when he came home from the war.

"Now we'll go a mile back to the south and you'll begin to see where the cotton is planted. It's our primary money crop. Just under five hundred acres. We depend on the rain and weather and that's as unpredictable as a woman according to Will," he said.

She didn't smile.

"That little house over there is where Will lived when he first came to work for my grandpa. That would have been more than forty years ago. He married and raised five kids in that house. They're all educated and hold responsible jobs. They married and left town to go to the big cities years and years ago. My dad hated the farm and took us to Huttig so he could work at the mill so Will and his wife moved into the house we'd had back then. It was closer to Grandpa and it worked out better that way."

He made a turn back toward the east. "This is the last leg of the four-mile trip, Alice. You've seen what I own but it'll be a fight to keep it for the next generation. I'm the only McNewel male still alive. That's why Grandma gave the farm to me. She left enough money for me to survive the winter and the cotton and tobacco crop brought in a good profit to get us a start next year. She says I'm not to go to the banks but to run the place on what I make from it. It's a scary thought."

One second he was talking, the next an explosion brought them to an abrupt halt, the following second a bolt of lightning shot from a dark cloud moving quickly in from the southwest and thunder rolled as if someone dumped a whole truckload of potatoes right on the top of the truck.

Everything stopped. The truck. Alice's heart. The blue skies.

"We just had a tire blow out," Ira said.

"So what do we do now?" Alice whispered.

"We got a choice. We can sit here until the storm blows over or we can make a dash back to Will's old house and hole up there until it's safe to walk back home. Should only be about a mile," he said.

"I vote for the house," she said. She'd never survive an hour or more of such close proximity to Ira, not without throwing her arms around him and kissing him. And then she'd feel like even a worse fool.

"Throw me that quilt. It'll be cold in there," he said.

She quickly unwrapped it from her legs, opened the door, and took off as fast as she could in a straight traveling skirt that all but hobbled her legs. She missed her overalls and work shoes. The high-heeled satin slippers she'd chosen to wear with her suit weren't worth a darn on ice with an approaching rainstorm on the horizon.

The living room of the small house was at least a little warmer than the outside weather; warm enough to fog up Alice's glasses. She shivered in spite of the warm wool coat she wore. Ira didn't even stop to look at her but went straight to the fireplace, threw in a few dry logs and kindling, and lit it with a match he found on the mantel.

"Hope there's nothing in the chimney to keep it from drawing."

Alice envisioned a smoke-filled room where she'd go running right back outside in the cold winter rain just to be able to breathe. Even that couldn't be any more difficult than the tightness in her chest as she watched him fiddle with the fireplace trying to make a warm room for her.

"Come close to the flame and I'll wrap you up in the quilt until it gets warm in here. It shouldn't take long even though the room is empty. Have a seat right here on the floor and take those wet shoes off. I bet your feet are freezing. Let me rub some warmth back into them," he said.

She obeyed and clenched her teeth to keep from gasping when he commenced to massaging her freezing feet. She wore cotton stockings but his touch was as hot as a branding iron. Combined with the heat from the fireplace she was soon shedding the quilt and her coat. Sweat beads that had nothing to do with the blaze in the fireplace formed on her forehead.

He removed his coat and hung it along with hers on a couple of nails inside the front door. "See, I told you it wouldn't take long to warm the place up."

"It's getting really cozy. Think the rain will stop soon?"

"Who knows? Will says we need all we can get this winter so it's welcome even if it did run us to drier ground."

"Ira . . ."

"Alice . . ."

They both started and stopped at the same time.

"You go first," he said.

"You answer my question first then I will. Why did you fire up so mad this morning? Were you really sweet on Sadie?"

"No, ma'am, I was never sweet on Sadie. I can't really explain why I got so mad. I was so eager to get to Huttig and then there was the misunderstanding. I know now why Mabel and Major kept telling me to go home. They knew you came here the same day I went there, but they could have told me that rather than beating around the bush. I was . . ." He almost poured out his heart to her but stopped. They were stuck in an abandoned house without even a chair to sit on until the storm passed. That could take hours and he didn't want to face the awkwardness that would fill the house if he admitted his feelings.

"I still don't understand but I need to explain something. It needs to be said even if it causes a heat wave right here in the middle of December. Cyrus all but proposed to me a few weeks ago. They came back through Huttig and —"

"Did you kiss him too?" Ira asked icily.

"No, I did not. He joined me on the porch the last evening they were at the hotel. He said he could stay in Huttig if I'd be willing to go to New York City for the holidays and live there, and there were art galleries where

I could show my work. He painted a pretty picture and said it was up to me whether he stayed or left the next morning. He said I just had to give him a reason to stay. I got the feeling he wasn't going to rush me but he needed something to hang on to. So I went to the cemetery . . ."

"The cemetery?" Ira frowned.

"Yes, at midnight, but then people don't harm crazies. It's bad luck. I'm safe to be out and about in the middle of the night. I talked to Momma and Daddy but no revelations about what I should do fell from the heavens or come up from the tombstones either."

"So what did you do?"

"I didn't give him a reason to stay. I simply kept to myself in my room until they were gone. Bridget gave them my good-byes and they left."

"Why? He's got so much to offer."

"I left the cemetery determined to take control of my life and forget you," she said bluntly.

Ira's blue eyes widened and his mouth dropped. "What did you just say?"

"I said I had to take control of my life and forget all about you. Evidently those kisses we shared didn't mean as much to you as they did to me. I've been attracted to you for years but you proposed to Catherine and then died. You know I never did believe you were dead. My heart didn't hurt like it would have if you'd been ripped away to eternity. The government said you were dead but down deep I just didn't believe it. I could have told Catherine that but I didn't. She would have thought it was just crazy old Alice and her silly ideas. And anyway, I wanted her to find someone else, just in case you did come home. I didn't want to see her with you and I dang sure didn't want you to be my brother. So I went home from the cemetery that night but I couldn't forget you. And then Sadie was marrying Lester and business is slow at Christmas so we decided to shut up the hotel a week until we could hire some help, and here I am. I've done what I came to do: make a complete fool of myself by throwing my heart at your feet. So now you can tell me that I'm like a sister to you and —"

"Don't you be telling me what to say, Alice O'Shea."

Will pounded on the front door. "Hello, the house. Y'all in there? I thought I might find you in here," he said as he hurriedly shut the door behind him and warmed his hands by the fire.

"What are you doing here?" Ira asked,

suddenly more irritated than he'd been all day. He'd been about to tell Alice how he felt and it dang sure wasn't sisterly love he had for her and now that had been thwarted.

"Come to rescue you two. Saw you leave out in that truck. Worked awhile in the barn on that old plow and y'all didn't make it back. So I checked the house and saw you'd left your breakfast on the table without eating it so I figured if you was holed up somewhere in the storm, you'd be gettin' hungry since it's on toward dinnertime now. Saw where the truck blew out a tire. We'll fix that tomorrow when the weather clears up. Right now, I expect you two better come on and let me take you back home in the buggy."

"Buggy?" Alice asked.

"That's right. Momma — that'd be my wife Pearl — and me always went to church on a Sunday in the buggy. Can't bring myself to get rid of it or the old mule that pulls it and it does come in handy ever so often, like today."

Alice set about putting her shoes and coat on. "Yes, it does, and thank you so much, Will. Would that mule take me to the train station after dinner?"

"It would, but it wouldn't be the right thing to do. Train leaves going north first thing every morning. Don't another one leave until tomorrow morning now. You'd be settin' there all night if I took you today."

Alice's heart sank. She'd have to spend another night in Ira's house with the heavy strange feeling lying between them like a fog in the tall pine country. She was tough and she'd endure; at least that's what she kept telling herself on the buggy ride back to the house.

"Have you had dinner?" Alice asked when Will had delivered them to the front door.

"No, ma'am, but I've got a pan of corn bread on the stove. That and some buttermilk will do for me," he said.

"Nonsense. Come on inside and sit by the fire with Ira while I stir us up something. You can eat with us," she said.

Will looked at Ira who nodded solemnly.

"Thank you, ma'am. I'll just put the old mule and buggy away and be right in," he said.

"Why'd you do that?" Ira asked Alice when they were inside.

"Because he rescued us and because he's probably hungry also." She hung her coat on the back of a chair and went straight to the kitchen. She found the same apron she'd tossed at the table that morning lying on the floor. She retrieved it and wrapped it around her waist, the strings making several rounds before she tied them.

She peeled potatoes and put them on to boil, sliced five healthy pieces from a ham, and readied them to fry in the morning bacon grease. She opened a jar of green beans and set them to boiling with two tablespoons of the bacon drippings. That would take fifteen minutes of hard cooking to prevent botulism. Then she made a pan of biscuits and shoved them into the oven.

"Smells good," Ira said. "Need any help?"

"You could throw out the leftovers from morning. Got a dog or a cat that might be interested?"

Ira scraped the plates into a pie pan in the corner and called, "Here kitty, kitty."

A black-and-white cat poked its head from the bedroom door and slithered around the walls toward the food dish.

"That's Scat," he said.

"Strange name."

"That's what I said when Grandma introduced us. Said the cat come up to the back door about six years ago. Wasn't nothing but a bag-of-bones kitten and she kept yelling 'Scat' at it. By the end of the day, the cat was here to stay and thought Scat was her name. She produces at least one litter of kittens every spring and Grandma says they're good mousers, to put them in the barn."

"Looks like Scat likes bacon and eggs even if they're cold."

"Grandma says she'll get used to me and will be a good house cat. That there won't be any mice in here if I let her stay. Reckon that's a small price to pay to keep the rats at bay."

"I said my piece back there. Now it's your turn whether I want to hear it or not," Alice said.

"Guess it is."

Will came through the door after the obligatory knock and claimed a chair next to Ira and the wood stove in the corner of the living room. "Smells like heaven in here. I'd swear Miz Mavis was back in this kitchen. She used to invite me to dinner sometimes and I loved her cookin'."

"Just fried ham, potatoes, and green beans with some biscuits. Didn't have time to make a pie or cake," Alice said.

"Then I'll eat an extra couple of biscuits with jam and call it dessert," Will said.

They sat together at the table in the kitchen, Will paying compliments with every other bite. Ira said little. Alice asked questions and was the perfect hostess.

"Looks like the rain has stopped. I'll get

on back out to the barn and spend the rest of the afternoon on that plow. I thank you for the good meal, Miss Alice, but most of all for the conversation. Old man like me and lonesome man like Ira here, we don't get to spend many midday meals at the table with a lovely lady," Will said.

"Thank you." Alice smiled.

"Ira, you might as well stay in this afternoon. Entertain Miss Alice here and we'll start afresh tomorrow morning after you take her back to the train station. If the truck can't be fixed by then, I'll hitch up the mule and the buggy," Will said.

Ira could have easily choked his best friend to death right at that moment. He couldn't tell Alice how he felt without stuttering and stammering like a schoolboy. Telling her was going to be embarrassing. Not telling her would eat at him the rest of his life. Will had interrupted twice now and then left on a note about taking her back to the train station. What a mess of a day!

"Well?" Alice asked from the other end of the table, leftovers and unspoken words sitting between them.

"I went to Huttig to see you, Alice. Not Sadie. I thought they were talking about you marrying Cyrus. Mabel came in the Black Swan to get Bridget's bouquet and the bride's veil. She just said the Rosenthals were there and I figured it was Cyrus and you. What would you have thought?"

"I can see where you'd make that mistake," she said.

"All the way home I figured you'd already married Cyrus and my heart hurt with the pain of losing you because I'd been so slow in declaring my feelings."

Alice cocked her head to one side. Surely she'd just heard wrong. The words were what she wanted to hear but what had he really said? "Really?"

"I've been in love with you for years."

"Then why did you propose to Catherine?"

He grimaced. "I don't think I can explain without making you so mad you'll be willing to stay in that train station all night."

"You better start trying or else I'll walk to town."

"I've never thought you were . . ." He paused.

"Thin on the intelligence?" she finished for him.

"No, I never did. But everyone else did and Catherine was so steadfast and so . . ."

"Smart?" She answered again.

"I asked her for all the wrong reasons and

I'm glad it didn't work out," he said in a rush.

"You are a very lucky man, Ira," Alice said.

"I don't feel so lucky today," he said. "I feel like a fool."

"Join the crowd."

"Would you marry me, Alice?" he blurted out.

Neither of them rushed across the room to embrace or share another kiss. The silence was so dense it couldn't have been cut with a machete. Then Alice spoke.

"When Baxter asked me to marry him I told him to ask me the next day at ten o'clock. I needed to kiss you and make sure all those fireworks from the first time weren't just a fluke. I did and it wasn't a fluke thing. Then when Cyrus wanted me to give him a reason to stay in Huttig he gave me the whole night to think about it. I thought about it all night but your name and face kept getting in the way. How long are you willing to give me?"

"As long as you need. I showed you what I have and can offer. It's more than I could offer when you fell on me that first day I was in Huttig. But it's not a big house in New York City where art galleries are. I still think you are talented and you'll be out here in a little bitty place with no outlet for your work. It's not an easy job you'll have, being the wife of a small-time cotton farmer, but I love you and I'll take care of you as best I can."

Alice bounded out of her chair and landed in his lap, almost overturning the rocking chair when she wrapped her arms around his neck and kissed him passionately.

"I've had all the time I need," she said breathlessly when they parted. "My answer is yes. And that's because I'm scared to death if I wait a minute you'll change your mind. Mine was made up years ago."

"Are you sure? Do you want a long engagement?"

"I want to be married to you and I want this to be my home. Is this afternoon too long? Yes, it is." She kissed him again. The fireworks were still there. "How about right now?"

He was afraid to let go of her for fear he'd wake up and find it was all a big dream. "But we can go to the Black Swan and you can have a big wedding like Sadie had."

"I've got an idea. Let's go find a marriage license and preacher tomorrow morning. I told Bridget I'd be back in a week because Catherine and Quincy promised to come home for Christmas Eve. We'll go see everyone and then come back home the day after

Christmas. If Will doesn't have family coming for the holidays, he can come with us."

"Alice, Will is colored," Ira whispered.

"So?"

"But he can't stay at the Black Swan. There'd be talk."

She threw back her head and laughed from the depths of her soul. "Honey, there's already talk. Who cares?"

Ira loved her more in that moment than he ever had.

"Tomorrow, then. Lord, this is going to be one long day and night," he moaned.

"Maybe. But tonight you stay at Will's. We are engaged and there'll be talk if you don't. I'm making a new start here and I'm not trading my village idiot reputation for one of a tainted woman."

Ira moaned again.

"I love you," she whispered into his ear.

Twenty-four hours never looked so long!

They stood before the Methodist preacher in an empty sanctuary the next day at one o'clock and said their wedding vows. The preacher's wife signed the license as one witness; Will signed as the other.

Ira carried Alice over the threshold of the door and shut the door with his foot when they were inside. He kept her in his arms all the way to the bedroom where he laid her on the bed.

"Alice McNewel, I can't promise to love you for your whole life but I will promise to love you for the rest of mine."

"That's the most beautiful thing I've ever heard." She smiled up at him. "Now kiss me again. I want to see if I see stars when I'm a wife."

He did.

And she did.

ABOUT THE AUTHOR

Award-winning author **Carolyn Brown** has written over thirty books. She and her husband, Charles, live in southern Oklahoma. In addition to writing she enjoys reading, travel and her family, which is a never-ending source of ideas. *From Thin Air* is her thirty-fifth book for AVALON and the second in the *Black Swan Historical Romance* series. *Pushin' Up Daisies, To Hope, To Dream, To Believe, The Dove, To Commit, To Trust, Evening Star, Sweet Tilly, Morning Glory, Promises, The PMS Club, Redemption, Chances, Trouble in Paradise, Absolution, Choices, The Wager, Augusta, Garnet, Gypsy, Velvet, Willow, Just Grace, Maggie's Mistake, Violet's Wish, Emma's Folly, Lily's White Lace, The Ivy Tree, All the Way from Texas, The Yard Rose, That Way Again, A Falling Star* and *Love Is* are also available.